JAN OTTERS' CLOSET

The Beginning

Kelly Forsyth-Gibson

authorHOUSE®

AuthorHouse™ UK Ltd.
500 Avebury Boulevard
Central Milton Keynes, MK9 2BE
www.authorhouse.co.uk
Phone: 08001974150

First published by AuthorHouse 12/7/2009

ISBN: 978-1-4490-5367-3 (sc)

This book is printed on acid-free paper.

For Ian, Lee and Ashleigh
I love you - Mum xxx

❧

ACKNOWLEDGMENTS

Alison Sage for the great editing – (thank goodness for you)
Iiris Kulomaa for the beautiful illustrations
and for baby Otso for giving mum time to do them

PROLOGUE

On a hilltop far across the Universe in the city of Zoogly, set against a beautiful orange and red sky, grew an amazing tree. Instead of having leaves, flames danced and flickered through its branches without burning the wood; the heat was so intense that few could get close to the tree. Its light shone from the hilltop like a beacon. However, the flames were not the only incredible thing about the Fire-Tree – for those who knew how to use it, it would grant wishes.

A red dragon by the name of Ouch knew all about the Fire-Tree; he had heard tales of it from his parents. He and his friends had long been suffering at the hands of the school bully, an angry and vicious fuzzbutt monster with three heads called Cruncher, Muncher and Walleye. It scared Ouch, picking on him and laughing at him all the time. Ouch dreaded the shrill of the school bell, knowing that at the end of the school day he and his friends were going to get pushed around and mashed by the bullying fuzzbutt. He couldn't tell anyone about it though – this would just make the fuzzbutt monster angrier than ever and lead to more pain and suffering for Ouch and his friends. But Ouch had had enough. It was time to take a stand and do something about it.

So Ouch had told his friends about the Fire-Tree and suggested that they should visit it to wish for a saviour, someone to come and help them deal with the bully.

Now they stood at the top of the hill with the blazing tree before them. Ouch was the only one who could approach the tree; the flames had no effect on his tough dragon skin. He took a branch from the tree and, taking it back to the others, they made their wish. Ouch crossed his fingers, hoping it would come true and that the Fire-Tree would send someone to save them. All they could do now was wait.

PART I

CHAPTER ONE

Trouble!

Ten year old Jan Otters sighed and hung her head as her mother scolded her yet again. She always seemed to be in trouble of some sort, both at home *and* at school. It wasn't deliberate and she didn't understand why it happened – she really wished she didn't cause so much bother. She just seemed to attract it because she didn't seem to fit in anywhere. She wanted more than anything to make her parents happy and proud, but it seemed beyond her.

Her mind drifted off, as it did so often to escape the harsh realities of her life – she would find all sorts of weird and wonderful thoughts drifting through her head. She couldn't stop them and they would often make her smile or laugh out loud – usually at just the wrong moment, so that she would find herself in trouble yet again.

Jan pulled her mind back to the present with difficulty. Her mother was shouting at her, "Jan Otters – one day they will lock you up and throw away the key, because you are so much TROUBLE!"

Jan didn't want to be locked up. In fact, she wished that she could travel and see the world. She had never been outside of the city where she lived and she knew there were wonderful things to see and do in other places.

Today, Jan was being told off for 'annoying' Lee, her fifteen year old brother. Jan often went into her brother's room, but she didn't mean to annoy him. She only ever wanted someone to play with, but he didn't seem to understand. Occasionally he would play a computer game with her, but usually he was too busy phoning his girlfriend to bother with Jan. He shouted, "Mum – tell the little pest to get out of my room and get back to her own planet!"

Jan and her family lived on the outskirts of the town in a little three-bedroomed farm cottage. There were no other children who lived nearby and very little for her to do, so Jan often got very lonely. And her imagination was her only companion.

Jan didn't even have her own space in the house any more. She used to have her own bedroom, which she had loved, but her grandmother had been in hospital recently and now lived with them. Jan had to give up her bedroom for Granma; although she missed it terribly she knew Granma needed it more because she wasn't well. Now Jan slept on the sofa in the living room.

Jan's dad often said that Granma was a 'feisty old bird', even after her accident. She had fallen at home and hit her head; she had been in a coma for a whole month and had to stay in hospital for a long time. When she woke up, she told Jan that her long sleep was filled with a dream about a fantasy world chock-full of the most amazing creatures. Sometimes, Jan would cuddle up beside her in bed and hear her tales of exciting adventures about these magical creatures that Granma had dreamt of. Jan loved this time and the stories of the magical creatures fascinated her. However, even these times were becoming fewer and fewer, as Granma wasn't feeling very well again and seemed to have a little bit less energy every day.

Trouble even followed Jan to her school. Mrs Whip, the head teacher, always said to her, "Jan Otters – what trouble have you caused now?"

But Jan didn't want to be in so much trouble. Instead she wished that she was the popular girl, the pretty girl, and the funny one that everyone in the class liked.

But one day at school, Jan's life was about to change forever!

Returning to school after the summer break, Jan was now in Primary Six. Jan's teacher was Miss Take. She was really nice, but she was quite young for a teacher and some of the children would take advantage of her inexperience. She would often fail to see that trouble was brewing till it was too late and then make a mistake as to who the trouble-causing child was. Since it always seemed to centre around Jan, she often got the blame.

On the first day back, Miss Take grouped the class into sets of four. Jan was upset to find she would not be sitting beside her only two friends in the world, Roland Ball and Lucy Small. Roland was a very clever boy who was a little self-conscious about his chubby tummy, and Lucy was a pretty girl but rather shy. She had cauliflower ears that stuck out and she was always trying to hide them behind her hair. Instead, Jan had to sit with Connor Edwards, who picked his nose and ate the contents right in front of you, Camilla Pitts, who was the posh princess of the class and who violently hated Jan and both her friends, and Camilla's best fried Sheila Gettem. Camilla, Sheila and their posse of bossy sidekicks made sure that every day at school, without fail, Jan, Roland and Lucy would be laughed at, picked on and hit.

That first day, Jan was tired because during the holidays she had been used to staying up late at night and sleeping later in the morning. Having to get up early was always such a nightmare on the first day back to school. She yawned as she listened to Miss Take talking about the work she wanted them to do and her mind began to wander. She began to slip into one of her daydreams.

Out of the corner of her eye, Jan could see Connor Edwards putting his finger up his nose and pulling out the most disgusting string of nasal slime she had ever seen! It was long green and sticky and he kept on stretching it, making it longer and longer. Jan's imagination took over and in her mind's eye the gloop got bigger and bigger, and then began to take on a life of its own. She imagined a huge head growing out of the end; it turned to face Connor and startled him by popping open two big eyes. Then, from nowhere, a large mouth opened up and grinned slowly at Connor. Suddenly, with one quick swoop the bizarre-looking substance catapulted towards the boy and bit his head off! For once, instead of Connor eating his gruesome nose package – it ate him!

Jan couldn't help herself; she began to roar with laughter at her thoughts.

Miss Take was furious. "Jan Otters!" she screeched.

Jan got such a fright from suddenly being wrenched out of her daydream that she began to fall backwards off her chair. She grasped at Camilla's chair to steady herself, but she caught Camilla's hair pleat instead, taking the squealing girl to the floor with her. "Ouch!" cried Camilla, holding her head in her hands and playing the situation for all she was worth, "Miss Take, she's nearly pulled all my hair out!"

However, out of sight of the young teacher, Camilla narrowed her eyes and gave Jan a sly, vengeful look.

"If looks could kill!" Jan thought, as she stood up. Camilla said quietly as she got up off the floor, "I will get you later for this match-stick head!"

"Oh for goodness sake," said Jan. "I didn't mean it!"

Miss Take ran over to Camilla and smoothed down her hair, making sure she wasn't hurt. Then she turned to face Jan and said angrily, "Jan Otters you silly girl, now look what you have done! Go and see Mrs Whip right now and explain your outburst to her."

Jan turned to leave the classroom, her heart sinking. She could feel the eyes of the class on her and hear Camilla and Sheila Gettem laughing at her. It was only 9.30 in the morning on the first day back to school and already she was in big trouble.

Jan dragged herself down the familiar corridor to the head teacher's office, wondering what would be in store for her this time. She knocked reluctantly on the head teacher's door, dreading what was to come.

"Come in", blasted the deep thunderous voice. "Ah, Jan Otters", the head teacher boomed as Jan peered around the door. "Well, what would the beginning of term be without a visit from you? I believe you have beaten last year's record by five minutes. So, what have you been up to this time?"

"It was my imagination again. I am dreadfully sorry," said Jan. "I just get thinking and…"

The head teacher's face contorted in a bitter expression as if she were chewing on dog doo doo. Mrs Whip was a long, tall lady; bending forward over her desk she loomed over Jan. Her grey hair was tied back into a bun and Jan always thought it was pulled back a bit too tight, leaving her face looking as if she was in total shock and disgust with the world around her. Jan had suffered herself in the past when her mum had pulled her own hair back too tightly into a pony tail and knew how it could hurt your head; she always thought this could be the reason why Mrs Whip was always so bitter.

"Oh, you were day dreaming again, so that makes it all right does it? Jan Otters, you have the attention span of a slug! I tell you, this year I am not putting up with it. Do you hear me?"

Jan stared miserably down at her shoes, trying to hide her eyes that were filling up with tears. Not wanting Mrs Whip to see her cry, she tried to think of something else to stop the tears from coming. With her overactive imagination running riot again, she began to imagine that the end of her shoes had big black Rottweiler dogs' heads on them. In her mind's eye, she could see the dogs barking, growling and foaming at the mouth as if they had a mad disease, struggling to pull away from Jan's shoes and trying to attack the petrified head teacher as she stood on top of her table screaming, "Get them away! Get them away!" Jan smiled at the thought.

"Are you listening to me girl?"

Jolted back to reality by the furious teacher, Jan could see that Mrs Whip's face was getting red with anger. As she got more worked up a purple hue joined in; the only good thing about the colours was that they almost hid the huge, black hairs growing out of her chin!

"Yes, I hear you Mrs Whip. I will get better; I promise," Jan told her dejectedly.

Jan was dismissed and told to go back to her class. On the way back, she wiped her eyes and sighed. She went into the girls' rest room to get some tissues and stopped for a moment to stare in the mirror. Her small, pale face stared listlessly back at her. Jan was not an ugly girl, but she felt she was rather plain. Her long, red hair was straggly and wild, and Jan hated it. It was full of curls that made it tuggy and difficult to brush; it hurt and Jan couldn't keep it under control so the other children made fun of it. They taunted her and sang: "Ginger headed carrot nose, pull the plug and away she goes."

Her gaze travelled down from her tangled hair to her shabby old skirt and her old shoes from last year. Jan's parents didn't have a lot of money, so Jan never had nice clothes. She wished her parents had a bit more, just enough to buy some new things. The bullies always teased her about her appearance, "Did you get your school clothes from a charity shop?" Of course Jan did, but she would never admit to this.

Sighing at the thought of having to return to the classroom and all the knowing looks passing between her classmates, Jan pushed the door open to leave the rest room and nearly jumped out of her skin as a face loomed towards her! However, it was only the school janitor facing her. He was holding a mop and bucket.

"Oh, hello Jan. Will you do me a favour? Go and put this back into my closet for me please. I have to run." He sighed and shook his head. "Max Winterbottom in class four has stapled his fingers to the desk again; I have to hurry."

And without another word he handed Jan the mop and bucket and took off.

Jan often passed the janitor's closet, but had never looked inside. Curiously, she opened the door. The room was dark but she could see it was tiny and could just make out the shelves full of 'fix-it things'. Jan was scared of the dark and small spaces, so she threw the bucket and mop into the closet hurriedly before closing the door quickly and turning around.

'Oh no!' thought Jan. Camilla Pitts and her sidekick, the aptly named Sheila Gettem, had just come around the corner of the corridor. They were walking towards her carrying the school register. It was too late for Jan to hide.

Camilla spotted Jan and asked, "Hey curly wurly, what were you doing in the janitor's closet? Up to no good are you Otters?"

Then Camilla whispered something to Sheila, and they exchanged an evil grin. They stepped closer and stretched out their arms quickly, each taking hold of one of Jan's arms. "Now," Camilla shouted to Sheila, "open the door!"

Sheila opened the door of the janitor's closet and they pushed Jan in roughly, closing the door and turning the key. She was locked in the cupboard. Her fear of small dark spaces getting the better of her, Jan panicked and threw her weight against the door, battering to be let out.

"Let me out! Please let me out. It's dark in here!"

But outside, Camilla just flicked Sheila a wicked smile and said, "Told you I would get her back!"

Jan was really scared now and began to cry. She tried to feel about in the dark amongst the unfamiliar shapes on the walls, looking for the light switch, but stumbled and tripped over the bucket she had thrown carelessly in earlier.

She threw her hands up to protect her head from bashing against the floor of the closet, but suddenly, instead of the sharp impact she expected, she felt herself falling, falling, falling through thin air! It was the strangest feeling, like a dream she often had of falling through miles of black space without hitting the bottom. Swirls of colour appeared and churned around Jan's head, making her feel giddy, and then everything swiftly came to a stop!

Jan put out her hands and, feeling something in front of her, she grabbed it to steady herself and stop her from losing consciousness. Gradually, her vision began to clear and whatever she was holding in her hands began, slowly, to move! Snapping quickly out of the moment she heard a voice say, "Let go of my tail will you!"

Blinking as she came back to full consciousness, Jan saw the long, red scaly tail she was holding slip out of her hands as a huge weight beside her shifted. Her heart began to beat faster. She looked up to where the voice was coming from and her eyes widened in shock and disbelief. There, looking down at her with smiling blue eyes, was a dragon!

CHAPTER TWO

A whole new world

"Wow!" Jan screeched, nearly jumping out of her skin. Her whole body froze and she stood staring in total disbelief at the large red creature in front of her. All the fairy stories she had ever heard with dragons in them came flooding into her mind – they only seemed to end well for the girl caught by the dragon when her handsome prince came to her rescue, but who was there to rescue Jan? Her face paled and she began to fill with terror.

Was she dreaming? The little girl's eyes were bulging out of her head and her body went limp with fear as she tried to edge back from the unbelievable sight. She could feel the heat from the dragon's body and smell smoke all around her.

"Well, are you coming to school?" The sound of the dragon's voice snapped Jan back to life.

"You *are* going to help me aren't you?" asked the dragon.

"H-h-help you with what?" Jan stammered. Then something occurred to her and her courage began to return. "Wait a minute," she said, straightening up slowly. "Dragons can't talk! What am I saying? Of course they can't, because there are no such things as dragons."

The dragon tilted his head to one side. "Well," he said, "if there are no such things as dragons then how come you've just landed in a pile of dragon poo?" He nodded in a satisfied fashion but then, realising the implication of what he had said, he quickly began to shake his head from side to side. "It's not mine, honest!"

Jan looked down. "Oh yuck, how gross," she yelped as she shook off a big pile of smelly muck from her shoe.

"Come on. Jump on my back, and we'll fly to school. Yup, yup, yup, that's the quickest way," said the dragon. "By the way, my name is Ouch, and I'm a dragon. What's your name, and what are you?"

"I know what's happened," said Jan. "Of course! I must have fallen on the floor in the janitor's closet after all, and hit my head. Yes, that explains it. I must be in a coma like Granma was, and I'm dreaming. There's no other explanation for it!"

Ouch shrugged. "Well, whatever works for you little, eh ... what are you anyway?" The dragon gave her a puzzled look and continued. "And stop being rude! Tell me your name."

"My name is Jan. Jan Otters, and I am a human."

The dragon bent down and reached out his scaly, clawed hand to shake Jan's hand. Jan hesitated, but deciding it was best to make friends, she offered him an unsure hand. After all, this was a dragon and it probably wasn't a good idea to make him angry!

"Very pleased to meet you, Jan Otters. Now get on my back, or we'll be late."

The dragon stood as tall as Jan's dad, and she was impressed with the magnificent purple wings folded neatly at his sides. He had a pale pinkish tummy, shading to darker red as it crept around his sides and then to a deep red at the back. What stood out most though were his huge bright blue eyes, firmly set with a thick black outline. Jan didn't quite know how she expected his scaly hide to feel; it looked as if it might be very slippery to sit on! As she climbed on to his warm back, she was surprised to feel that it was dry and very comfortable; as she settled into place she determined to go along with this dream. After all, it wasn't every day that a girl got to fly on the back of a dragon!

"So where am I, Ouch?" asked Jan, giggling at the creature's name.

The dragon looked back at Jan over his shoulder. "You're on a butterfly planet, and our city is called Zoogly," he replied.

"All right," Jan said as she rolled her eyes, "Whatever... But why are you called Ouch?"

"Well, that's a funny story," said the dragon. "You see, according to my parents, six weeks after I was born, I was breaking out of my egg shell. My mum was so excited that when she bent down to kiss my face, she blew out a flame from her mouth by accident and it sizzled my eyelashes. So my first word was 'Ouch!'"

Ouch explained to Jan that, according to dragon tradition, since a baby dragon can speak as soon as it's born, the first words that a hatchling utters becomes his or her name.

"Oh, I see," laughed Jan, as the dragon took off into the sky.

Terror and excitement ran through Jan in equal measure as she was carried up into the clouds. The warm wind blew her bronze hair around her face, and she held on tightly to the dragon's neck as she looked around in awe at the beautiful orange and red sky. She gazed down and thought how amazing her coma was! She saw a land full of castles, towers, mountains and lakes that stretched on for miles. "Whoa!" Jan said out loud.

As they flew higher and higher into the sky, Jan could not believe what she was seeing! The entire city really *was* riding on the back of an enormous, beautiful butterfly!

Looking at the land below, Jan thought that this must be like the view from an aeroplane window. Far away in the distance, beyond the city of towers, turrets and the surrounding countryside, she could just make out the edges of the giant butterfly's wings. The multi-coloured insect flapped its wings very slowly, sending a warm wind wafting throughout the kingdom. Although it was flying, it appeared to be floating in space. The colourful sky, unlike on earth, ended several miles above the horizon and above that, black space began, sprinkled with brilliant stars like dewdrops in bright sunlight. Jan looked past the stars and was amazed to see other spectacular planets all around her. 'This is so cool,' she thought.

"Ouch, did you say we were going to a school?" bellowed Jan, her mind coming back to her companion.

"Yes", said Ouch. "You are going to stop the bullies from hurting me and my friends!"

"What?" Jan exclaimed in disbelief.

"Yes. My friends and I wished at the Fire-Tree for someone to come and help us with our problem, and it sent you," explained Ouch.

Jan was stunned and asked Ouch what exactly he had wished for and what he expected her to do. Ouch said that he and his friends were being bullied by a three-headed pupil at their primary school, a fuzzbutt monster. It made Ouch's life a misery, teasing him and his friends and pushing them around every single day. Sick of this treatment, Ouch and his two friends had finally plucked up the courage to do something about it, so they had made a wish at the magical Fire-Tree for someone to come who would be able to deal with a situation like theirs and it had sent Jan. Ouch continued to tell her all about Cruncher, Muncher and Walleye, the names of the fuzzbutt's three heads. He explained that fuzzbutts usually only had two heads, so everyone at Zoogly Primary thought this monster was horrible because it looked so different.

Cruncher was the leader, and he had the head of a large bull with horns, a big hoop ring in his nose and red eyes. Muncher was the middle brother, who had a head of broccoli with eyes and a mouth. Jan asked Ouch why Muncher had broccoli for a head, and Ouch explained that it was because Muncher was vegetarian. Fuzzbutts normally only have a meat-eater head and a vegetarian head, but this fuzzbutt was a mutant. The third head, Walleye, was a Zoogly.

Zooglies were round in shape, about half the size of a small girl like Jan. They had a shock of fuzzy, lime green Mohican hair, short necks and little thin arms. A Zoogly could be born into a mixer monster like a fuzzbutt, but it was rare. This fuzzbutt in particular had a really vicious streak. Some said that it was dropped on its heads at birth, and Walleye came off the worst for it. That would account for how weird he was. One of his eyes would look *at* you while the other one would whiz all over the place.

Cruncher and Muncher both had long necks with strong arms in contrast to Walleye's short neck and spindly arms, and all three brothers were attached to a big, fat, dark green body the shape of a hairy slug. Altogether, the fuzzbutt was the size of a large car, and it was very angry.

As they flew onwards, Ouch explained much more about the planet and its inhabitants. There were many different kinds of creatures on the planet including fuzzbutts, dragons and unicorns, but the population was mainly made up of Zooglies. Ouch and his friends attended Zoogly Primary school, and amazingly, they were all about the same age as Jan.

While Ouch was relating all this to Jan, she could see a magnificent stone building with a huge pointy tower approaching. Ouch landed outside it, next to a sign that read:

Zoogly Manor School
Assurance of a 1st class education for your children,
or you can send them back for free or eat them!

Jan read the sign and thought how strange all this was. "I can't just walk into your school. Won't they wonder where I've come from? Have they ever seen a human before?"

Ouch seemed to give this some thought before he replied, "I don't think so, but it's OK. Nothing is strange here. They'll just think you're an exchange pupil from one of the other planets." And with this, he pulled Jan in through a crack in the wall, right into a black floating classroom. Jan glanced round the room. It was all pitch black, like the space above the city but without the brilliant stars and planets. It was set up like a normal classroom with tables, chairs and a blackboard, but unlike on Earth they all floated in space without anything to hold them up! Jan shook her head, marvelling at it.

"Hurry, catch a seat, and sit here beside me." Ouch pointed to a floating desk and chair.

Suddenly, a magic door appeared from nowhere and slowly opened. All at once, the most amazing and weird creatures that she could ever have imagined started to pour through. The noise was deafening as they walked in. There were creatures grunting, squealing and sobbing, and Jan was sure she could hear one of them singing opera while another was passing wind!

Immediately, a loud voice said, "Sit down, class, and be quiet!"

"That must be the teacher," Jan thought to herself.

As she looked round, she saw a whirling blue and silver cloud float into the room, with small beady eyes and a wiggly mouth. Each time the cloud spoke it was like thunder, and it held a bolt of lightning like a walking stick.

Ouch leaned over to Jan. "That's Mr Smith; he's from Control Freak Spectrum – that's where all our teachers come from."

Jan began to chuckle.

"Shhhhh….don't make a noise, or you'll get hit by a bolt of lightning and sent to Mrs Floater, the Head Teacher," whispered Ouch.

A loud crash drew Jan's attention back to the door, just in time to see a creature that could only be Cruncher, Muncher and Walleye stomp in. Jan almost wet herself with shock!

The fuzzbutt monster smashed its way through the tables and sent everyone floating wildly around the room.

"These are our seats!" yelled the monster. And with that, the huge fuzzbutt sat down across from Ouch and Jan, rudely taking up five seats. Cruncher, the bull, looked over to Ouch and ran his finger across his neck, then pointed it towards Ouch.

The young dragon gulped with fear and slid down to hide behind Jan. Despite feeling very out of place, the little human couldn't help but feel that there was something very familiar about all of this, even if it was in the most bizarre situation.

Muncher also began to stare. He whispered something to Walleye, and they both gawked at Jan. Walleye squeezed his eyes closed, then he popped them open quickly and his pupils went all over the place. He started to make a strange whooping noise, and his long tongue flapped all around his face.

"Strange," thought Jan.

"Right!" bellowed Mr Smith, the cloud teacher. "Tonight, as you all know, is the Zoogly main street parade, and I need you all to make a fly chain, which as you know, will be unbreakable once the last link is sealed. So at break time, I want you to catch as many flies as you can. Stick them behind your ears, and whoever gets the most can eat the leftovers after we make the chain decorations. Do I make myself clear?"

A chorus of "Yes, Mr Smith," rang out.

"Good, then I will take the register." As the teacher shouted out the names, Jan looked in astonishment at each of her new classmates, thinking to herself that this was the strangest dream she had ever had and hoping against hope that her new classmates would all be as friendly as Ouch!

CHAPTER THREE

A funny lot

"Rupert Dangleworth!" shouted Mr Smith.

"Here," said a voice, but when Jan looked over it disappeared. "No, sorry, here Mr Smith." And the pupil disappeared again.

"Stay still, Rupert Dangleworth, or I will send a thunder call to your parents."

Ouch had told Jan that when they were growing up, all Zooglies had issues, and their strange behaviour could easily turn into a habit. Rupert, it turned out, was a vanishing Zoogly and each time he got nervous, he vanished and reappeared somewhere else.

"Oops!" shouted Mr Smith.

"Here," cried a pretty and cuddly blue dragon with beautiful yellow eyes and long, black eyelashes.

"Why is she called Oops?" Jan whispered to Ouch.

"Because that's the first word she said. She ate her brother by mistake, and her mum gave her a row," replied Ouch.

Jan smiled and shook her head, thinking that this was all very crazy but very funny.

"Arty Farty!" shouted Mr Smith.

Arty was a clever and cheerful bookworm, who was a foreign exchange student to Zoogly. When he spoke he made the strangest, windy noises out of his mouth. These peculiar sounds were produced in long bursts for a couple of words, and when he had a long sentence, only the sound of a single 'parp' came out. Only the teacher and a few of Arty's friends could translate.

"Prrrph, squeak, parp, trrrrrrrrrrrrrrrrrrrrrrrrrrrrrrr, crack." Then his sentence tailed off with a sound like the noise of a slow-leaking balloon.

A cloud of purple air surrounded everyone in the class as he finished speaking, and coughs and cries of "peeugh" erupted. Arty suffered from very bad breath.

"Quiet down everyone. Must we go through this every time Arty Farty says that he is here?" Mr Smith shouted. "Now, Jilly Wobbleton?"

"Here," wobbled Jilly who was, for want of a better description, a jelly with wings!

"Rain-bow Hyde White?" asked Mr Smith.

"Here Mr Smith," sobbed Rain-bow.

Jan looked to the side and saw the most beautiful white pony. She had gorgeous, soft, feathery wings and a large red bow on her head, which rained pretty coloured droplets of water. Ouch told her that Rain-bow was waiting to become a unicorn, but the unicorn horn wouldn't grow until her bow stopped raining tears. This always upset Rain-bow, but unbeknownst to her friends, her tears held magical powers that turned anything bad into ice for a few minutes. She had never told anyone this, because unicorns are very peaceful creatures and shy away from disagreements. She didn't want to be caught up in any fights!

"Opreea Bigmouth!" shouted Mr Smith.

Opreea began to sing along with her imaginary orchestra. "I am heeeeeeeeeere, Mr Smith, it's so cleeeeeeeeear, Mr Smith. Now all cheeeeeeeeer, Mr Smith!"

Opreea Bigmouth was a girl Zoogly, and she would rather sing opera than speak. It was a phase she was going through.

Time passed quickly as Jan strained to check out each of the funny-looking pupils she was now sharing a class with. For the first time that she could remember, what was happening around her was more than enough to hold her attention; she had gone fully half an hour without daydreaming and getting into trouble!

The register call was finally finished, and Mr Smith looked at her and said, "And just who are you? Where is your fish tail? Why don't you have fins on your back and what's all that attached to your tummy?"

"I'm a human," explained Jan, "and these are my legs."

The teacher puzzled hard over this for a moment before he told her, "Well I have only ever seen something like you at Star Lake before. How extraordinary. Oh well, give me your name for the register."

"My name is Jan Otters, sir."

Everyone looked at Jan and made faces at her attempt to show politeness and respect toward the teacher.

Mr Smith's long wiggly mouth broke into a large smile. "Well, welcome to Zoogly Primary School, Jan, and mind you behave yourself in my class."

"Yes, sir," replied Jan, relieved not to be shouted at for once. She felt as if she had finally found a place where she wasn't the weirdest one in class!

Mr Smith then told everyone that they would have to take it in turn to read their poems, written over the weekend, to the class. "So," asked Mr Smith, "who is going to read out their poem first?"

Arty Farty sprang up and nearly hit the teacher right between the cloud eyes.

"All right Arty, off you go."

Then everyone held their noses as Arty said, "Blip!"   The students brushed the blinding purple air away from their faces, and Mr Smith said that he would translate. He cleared his vocal cords by coughing thunder and began.

"Now listen, everyone. I will now tell you what Arty said;

Arty Farty had a party

And all his class mates were there

His cousin, Tutty Fruity, let out a beauty

And they all required air!"

Everyone began to laugh and roll around, including Arty, who also made the sound of a drum roll.

"That is so funny!" laughed Jan. Then, the shrill of the bell made her jump.

"All right, everyone, time for break" said Mr Smith. "Off you all go and remember to catch those flies!"

Outside it was warm. Jan looked up and saw two moons in the sky; one red and one blue. It was still hard to believe that she was now standing in a city that was on the back of a bug.

The playground was buzzing with all kinds of crazy characters, and for once, she did not feel like the odd one out. Playtime at Zoogly Primary School was fun and the little newcomer laughed and messed around with her new friends. But this happiness was about to change very quickly.

Behind her, she could hear, "THUD-SLIDE! THUD-SLIDE! THUD-SLIDE!"

Jan watched as her classmates scattered in all different directions, tearing through the playground to find a safe hiding place.

'This cannot be good,' she thought. She looked over her shoulder. It was Cruncher, Muncher and Walleye.

"So the little human wants to be friends with the wrong bunch does she?" blasted Cruncher into Jan's face. The hideous monster swiped at Jan and tried to grab her. But Jan jumped back out of the way in horror and, thinking that nothing could happen to her in a dream, she said with more courage than she would have had in 'real' life, "Why are you picking on me?"

Muncher, the broccoli head, stared at Jan and said in a haughty taughty voice, "Personally, I don't want anything to do with you. I am a vegetarian you see, so although my brothers will eat you, don't blame me!"

"Oh yes, make no mistake, we will eat you!" whooped Walleye. He turned to Cruncher and said, "But let's torment her first by calling her names and laughing at her!" They started to call her names, picking on her looks, laughing and sneering at her.

15

From behind a tree in the playground, Ouch, Rain-bow and Arty peered around to see what was happening. Then they all slid back to hiding in shame.

"At least they are giving us a break from being bullied," sobbed Rain-bow.

Gaining courage and not allowing herself to dwell on the fact that she was facing the bully alone as everyone else hid, Jan looked up at the three-headed bully and raised her voice, "Do you really think that makes you clever, saying all that silly stuff? Hasn't anybody ever told you?" she shouted, "IT'S NOT JUST BROKEN BONES THAT CAN HURT, NAME CALLING HURTS TOO!" And with that, she walked away as the bell rang.

As she walked into class, she met up with Ouch, Arty and Rain-bow. Ouch was skipping and jumping up and down. "Oh, you were so brave. I knew you would help us," the excited dragon said triumphantly. The young dragon was very clumsy on the ground though and tripped over his big feet! The fuzzbutt monster had sneaked up behind them as they made their way into the classroom, and Cruncher took advantage of this. He grabbed Ouch in a headlock and thumped his enormous arm down on the poor dragon's head.

"Nobody will help you, dragon, and after school we are going to tear you and your friends apart!" he growled ominously.

Cruncher let go as soon as he saw the teacher coming towards the door. Ouch ran behind his friends, shaking uncontrollably.

Jan knew this feeling only too well and wished there was something she could do. But with a sinking heart she thought how could she possibly help Ouch, Arty and Rain-bow when she couldn't even solve her own bullying problem back at her own school?

CHAPTER FOUR

The big fight!

It was nearing the end of the school day, and the class had free play time. Mr Smith was outside hanging the fly chain that they had made out to dry, so Jan went over to Ouch, Arty and Rain-bow. "I'm having a blast here, learning about all your different planets, but making those chain decorations with dead flies is just sick and wrong," she laughed.

Her three new friends just sat there looking very miserable.

"Why do you all look so unhappy?" Jan asked.

"Because we are all going to get mashed after school, of course," Ouch said, trembling.

Jan sat down beside them, resting her head in her hands. She had been having such a good time that she had forgotten all about the bullies. "I've got it," she said. "We have a saying on Earth that two heads are better than one. The fuzzbutt has three heads so, if we all put our heads together, that makes four! Together, we can come up with a plan to beat it."

A flicker of hope came across their faces as she told them from her own experience, "When bullies strike, they usually gang up and pick on one person. Maybe if friends all stick together, it might be enough to scare the mean fuzzbutt off. It can't come after all of us!"

"But we're no match for Cruncher, Muncher and Walleye. Have you seen the size of that thing?" cried Ouch.

"Not to mention its strength," said Rain-bow.

Jan looked down at her shoes and went quiet.

Just then, Arty said, "Parp!"

"What did he say?" Jan asked Ouch, as she fanned the purple smog away.

Ouch explained that sometimes Arty's dead ancestors would send helpful riddles to his head. They had just said:

"We should fight fire with fire, cloud the situation

and put our enemies on ice!"

"But what does it mean?" asked Rain-bow.

"I'm not sure," said Jan, "but I do know this. We should not give up so easily. We should stick together and show those big bullies that we now have a 'BIG-JOINED-TOGETHER-VOICE' and we are not going to put up with it any more!"

"Ahhh," Ouch screamed as the bell went off. All four of them turned round to see where the fuzzbutt was.

Cruncher, Muncher and Walleye each took it in turn to grin slowly at them. Cruncher curled up the knuckles of one hand and started punching his other hand hard with it.

"Oh no," squealed Rain-bow, as the teacher ushered them out of the classroom.

Everyone spilled out to the playground. They all knew about the beating that was about to take place, and the rest of the class considered it a spectator sport!

All four friends stood together facing Cruncher, Muncher and Walleye. Ouch swallowed hard; he looked up at Cruncher and, summoning all his courage, he said nervously, "You'd be expecting us to make a run for it, but we've decided that you are not going to bully us anymore!" Ouch looked at his friends for encouragement, and they all nodded in agreement.

Cruncher began snorting at this show of defiance, Muncher looked totally indifferent to the situation and Walleye began to chant, "Ouch, Ouch, Ouch!", smacking his little hands together all the while. The shivering dragon looked at all three fuzzbutt heads and cringed in terror. How was he going to escape this?

Seeing the huge creature's body start to pull back to gain momentum for an enormous attack, Ouch's courage finally failed and he whirled around, looking for somewhere to run. The dragon knew he was being cowardly and gave his friends an apologetic glance, but the prospect of a painful beating was too much for him. As fast as his robust body could take him, Ouch ran and ran and ran. The sudden abundance of nerves affected his usual perfect flying take-off and with this skill compromised, he just couldn't fly away. Five rounds of the playground and still the relentless three-headed monster pounded after the breathless dragon.

Cruncher, Muncher and Walleye's body was not athletic by any means, but what it lacked in speed, it more than made up for in the length of the "caterpillar-like" strides it could make. It kept up easily with Ouch, not allowing him to slow for a second.

Ouch's big clumsy feet always let him down when he was on the ground and in his haste to run faster while he grew more and more tired, he inevitably tripped over. His long reptilian body crashed to the ground and slid to a halt near his friends, but not before taking in every bump and stone on the ground. Evil laughter bellowed behind him as the large slug-like trio caught up with him.

Trembling terribly and in some pain, Ouch looked up and feared for the next moment of his life. In fact, everyone in the playground feared for the next moment of his life!

After a dreadful pause that seemed to go on forever, the three-headed fuzzbutt's fat tail suddenly whipped through the air from nowhere, battering Ouch and further flattening him into the ground. Cruncher's strong arms followed, hammering heavily through the air as he shouted to his brothers to join in by getting the others.

Muncher looked around for the opportunity to create more mayhem and, seeing that Rain-bow was about to fly away, he reached out quickly and grabbed her by the tail. He swung her round and round, high above his head, as she whinnied for help. Deep in shock and frozen with terror, she was unable to rain the freezing tears that could save her!

"Quick," growled Cruncher to Walleye, "grab that bookworm!"

Walleye stretched out his thin little arms and, wrapping his sticky little fingers around Arty's neck, snatched him up off the ground.

Jan watched in horror as her new friends were tortured by the big nasty bully. She felt totally helpless. Oh, what had she done getting them all to stand up for themselves like that? She was on the verge of tears. While the monster was totally occupied with her friends, she was free to think and knew how important this was. All her friends' energy was taken up with trying to cope with the mashing they were getting at the hands of the fuzzbutt. But how could she possibly help? There had to be something she could do!

Then, she remembered about Arty's riddle. "Oh think, think!" she cried, wracking her brains, "what were those words?"

"We should fight fire with fire, cloud the situation

and put our enemies on ice!"

"That's it!" shouted Jan, suddenly seeing a solution. She ran over to where Ouch was being held captive. "Quick, Ouch," Jan said, "use your fire breath to get free."

Ouch looked puzzled, then his eyes opened wide as he realised what Jan was asking him to do. Desperately, he took a big breath and blew out a huge flame that sizzled along Cruncher's arm. Cruncher howled in pain and immediately released Ouch. The frightened dragon jumped up from his confined position and ran over to Jan.

Jan turned to the dangling bookworm and shouted, "Arty, say something!"

Arty nodded his squished head and began to make the kind of drum noises that are usually produced from a person's bottom. The air was suddenly thick with a blinding purple cloud.

Muncher cried, "I'm blind, I'm blind, I can't see anything!" as he let go of Arty, dropping him to the ground.

"Arty, quick, over here!" cried Jan.

Walleye was still swinging Rain-bow above his head; Jan looked around in frustration for something to hit him with. Spying a fallen tree branch, she scooped it up, ran over to Walleye, jumped up and hit his arm with it as hard as she could.

"That hurt!" moaned Walleye as he released his grip on Rain-bow. Seeing that Rain-bow was free, Jan fled back to her friends and watched as the young filly's outstretched wings took flight. She flew over to her friends, where they all stood exhausted and trembling. A very angry three-headed monster glowered at them.

"I don't understand the last piece of the riddle," Jan said, shaking her head anxiously. "I know that *fight fire with fire* had to come from Ouch and *cloud the situation* had to come from Arty, but *put your enemies on ice*? What's that all about?"

Rain-bow bowed her head down to reach Jan's ear and, sobbing, she said, "Jan, I have never told anyone this but my tears are magical; they can freeze bad things. Maybe that's the ice thing?"

Jan's eyes opened wide and she hugged the pony. "Rain-bow, that's it! That's the missing piece of the message! Now this would be a very good time to throw one of those magic tears onto that big hairy monster who is storming towards us!"

Having seen her friends deal with the monster and escape in their own ways, the proud pony wasn't frozen any more. With Jan to encourage her, she flicked her head and a blast of blue and gold water shot across onto the monster. Immediately, spears of bright light showered all around, almost blinding everyone. Slowly, the light faded and everyone turned their eyes to the fuzzbutt.

It was frozen solid.

CHAPTER FIVE

Tame the monster

A large angry statue, with three frozen faces, filled the playground. Ouch, Arty and Jan were about to start celebrating their great victory, but Rain-bow stopped them.

"The magic will only last for a few minutes," she told them quietly. "We have to get out of here!"

For a moment, an eerie silence filled the playground, followed by the gradual eruption of noise. All kinds of creatures came out of hiding to congratulate the now famous friends who had defeated the nastiest bully in Zoogly.

"Hooray!" Cheers celebrating the conquest rang out, but at any moment, the friends knew that the monster would defrost and be more horrible than ever!

Jan looked above her and caught sight of the fly chain decoration that the class had made that afternoon. It was hanging over the branches of a tree, and she remembered the teacher's words from earlier, "...will be unbreakable once the last link is sealed."

"Quick!" Jan told her friends urgently. "Let's get the fly chain and wrap it around the fuzzbutt." The other three looked at each other.

"Now!" shouted Jan. "Before it's too late!"

Ouch flew high to the top of the tree and tugged at the chain. He flapped his purple wings hard as he struggled to free the chain and release it to the ground. Rain-bow, Arty and Jan caught it and wound the chain around the monster's waist, pulling it tight.

"Now what?" asked Rain-bow.

"Now," said Jan, "we have to hoist this big meanie up to the top of the tree before it can do any more harm!"

Ouch soared back to the highest part of the tree. He hovered as he wrapped the chain around a thick, strong branch, then landed beside his friends with the other end. Holding a section of the chain each, they all began to pull, but they could only lift the monster slightly. Out of the corner of her eye, Jan could see Cruncher's head starting to move; Ouch jumped in fright, letting go of the chain.

The fuzzbutt thudded back to earth with a crash. "Woooooe," everyone gasped.

Then suddenly, Walleye's hand began to move.

"We'll never make it!" shouted Jan. "They're too heavy and they're thawing fast!"

Suddenly, the chain pulled through all of their hands with ease, and the monster was hoisted up swiftly to the top of the tree. Jan looked over her shoulder in bewilderment.

All of the school creatures were behind them, pulling at the chain. Jan was overwhelmed with the help and support that everyone was giving to each other.

Victory! The deed was done and they all looked up to the dangling fuzzbutt. A very angry Cruncher looked down. "You wait until we get free!" he growled, head butting and punching the air in a vain attempt to break the chain.

The four friends looked at each other. "What will we do now?" asked Rain-bow. "They can't stay up there forever, and they'll still get us when they get loose," she sobbed.

They all clustered around Jan, looking for an answer. Jan was ready for them. "We are going to talk with them," said Jan, "and tell them how they make us feel."

Oops, the very girly blue dragon said, "But they won't listen to us!"

To which Jan replied, "Well, they don't have any choice in the matter at the moment. They can't go anywhere; we have the upper hand for once. They'll have to listen!"

Confusion filled the air, and they all looked at each other for some kind of explanation. Jan asked everyone to gather round and sit below the tree. There, they could all take a turn to tell the bullies how they made each of them feel. To begin with, Cruncher, Muncher and Walleye just laughed at the accusations. However, Jan told the crowd that the bullies were not getting down until they realised how bad their behaviour was, so they must continue.

After many acts of cruelty and torment were discussed, Jan slowly began to reveal her own feelings to the fuzzbutt. She looked up and told the brothers that back home, where she came from, every day she had to face a small group of people who made her life a total misery. "It hurts," she said. "It's cruel and the hitting, especially, causes agony and deep feelings of hopelessness." She recalled one of the bullies, who taunted her friend by name-calling and laughing, just because she had 'cauliflower ears'. She explained how it made her friend cry every day.

Muncher hung his head, and Jan thought she heard him speak softly. "Did you say something Muncher?" Jan asked.

"Yes." Muncher started to speak up. "I don't like looking different. I'm stuck in the middle and I have a broccoli head. I know everyone laughs at me!"

Jan reassured him that nobody was laughing at him. For one thing, everyone was too scared of him and his brothers to ever laugh at them.

Then Walleye spoke up and said he was sorry for all the bad things he had done to his classmates. He blamed it on his 'issues' phase but he would try and behave from now on.

Then everyone looked at Cruncher, who simply glared back at them.

Jan was relieved that Muncher and Walleye were able to understand the heartache they had caused, but Cruncher was going to need a bit more convincing. She told him about Camilla Pitts being the leader of a bunch of dreadful bullies back home and how they would ruin Jan's life by picking on her every day, often making her feel sick with nerves.

Cruncher crossed his arms, huffed and said, "Well, if you think I'm going to change you can think again! It's not as if you would all start to come over and hang out with us, or invite us to come to your birthday parties, is it? Let's face it, you all hate me, and I hate you lot!"

"But we don't hate you. It's just that you're always taking the mickey," someone shouted.

"We're just scared of you," another said.

"I would play Hoop-The-Moon with you," the blue dragon insisted. "Yeah, you would be good on our team. With your height you would definitely win the gold moon trophy for us!"

Ouch loved the game and always wanted to be in the team, but the big-footed numpty was very clumsy and had even been known to fall over a chalk line drawn in the playground!

"I want to play, I want to play!" He blasted out with great enthusiasm. He jumped up and down, landed on the side of his foot and fell backwards over his tail, ending up flat on his back.

Ouch lay still for a moment, then looked up at all the stunned faces, including those of the dangling fuzzbutt. He shrugged his shoulders and, giggling, he said, "So I suppose I won't make a good ballet dancer!"

Suddenly, something happened that Jan thought she would never see. Joining in with everyone else, Cruncher began to laugh, a real big belly laugh.

But this time, it was not *at* his classmates; it was *with* them.

CHAPTER SIX

I want to go home now

Cruncher, Muncher and Walleye were steadily lowered to the ground. Everyone felt sorry for them, and it seemed that the three brothers finally understood how they were making others feel. The fly chain was unwrapped and the three heads slowly looked over the sea of understanding faces. Cruncher, Muncher and Walleye huddled together and whispered.

"Listen carefully everyone!" Muncher called out. "We have decided that we will stop all this bullying on one condition."

"And what is that?" asked Jan.

"Cruncher wants to be the captain of the Hoop-the-Moon shooting team," said Muncher.

A huge sigh of relief swept over everyone, and they all agreed that he could be. It wasn't the best of starts, issuing ultimatums, but it was a move in the right direction towards peace and possible friendship.

In this strange place that seemed so different from home, Jan was able to see the bullies as they really were, and had finally understood something. She told Ouch that the fuzzbutt just needed to be part of something and feel needed.

Surprisingly, Cruncher bent down to Jan and said, "Thank you."

Jan didn't say anything. She just looked up and flashed him a smile.

Ouch came over and hugged Jan. "Thank you, Jan. We needed someone to help, and you really have come through for us. I don't know about you, but I feel more confident now. Well, I guess that's easy to say *now*, now that it's all over, but you know what I mean. Anyway, I need you to know this Jan. You will always be my friend."

Jan looked up into Ouch's eyes, stood on her tip toes, held his face in her hands and smiled. "I have had the most brilliant adventure ever, and I have made some wonderful new friends, but I miss my mum and dad and want to go home now please."

Rain-bow's ears pricked up. "Don't go Jan. Stay here with us. "We will have so much fun. You will just love the picnic area at the edge of Fairy Forest, and I wanted to swim in Star Lake with you. Don't you think it's beautiful here?"

Jan could feel the tears begin to sting her eyes. "But I miss my home and..." Jan shook her head as if to clear it. "What am I saying? None of this is real. I'm in a coma, but how do I wake up? I wish Granma had told me that!"

All eyes were on Jan.

Ouch said, "I don't know what a coma is Jan, but I think I know a way you could get home."

"How?" asked Jan.

"Well, we made a wish at the Fire-Tree for you to come here, so that means we can wish for you to go home too," said Ouch.

"Oh, that would be wonderful!" said Jan.

She said goodbye to the class, and spent a few moments talking to Cruncher, Muncher and Walleye. She told them that the class had accepted them now and they could be friends, but they would have to be careful not to go back to their bullying ways or everyone would stop speaking to them again.

"I'm ready now," said Jan, and the four friends set off for the Fire-Tree.

"I really wish you could have met my mum and dad," said Ouch. "My mum is expecting a batch of new, baby dragon eggs next year. We would have fun watching them hatch and saying their first words." He giggled.

Jan looked up at him and reached for his hand.

Ahead, she could make out a hill and standing tall on the top was the most amazing tree she had ever seen. Orange and yellow flames glowed brightly through the branches. It was breathtaking. It was the Fire-Tree.

Together the friends pushed on through the countryside and up the slopes of the hill. As they climbed up the last part, Rain-bow turned to Jan and said, "Oh, I wish you could come with me to Unicorn Island. Our land is at its best when the sun sets and the warm Zoogly wind softly whispers throughout the kingdom. You can see the grass dancing in the fields and the sand blowing around in little blizzards by the edge of the crystal clear lake. And you know what; we're going to have a huge party when my horn grows, which with a bit of luck shouldn't be long now."

Jan ran her hands through Rain-bow's silky mane and told her that she would be an outstanding unicorn.

Jan imagined all the fun she could have with her new friends, but she knew she desperately wanted to see her mum, and to tell Granma all about her amazing dream.

"What an awesome adventure this had been," she thought. It was her best dream ever, and she had learnt a lot. She decided, when she awoke from her strange journey, she would handle the bullies at her own school. It was time and she knew just what to do.

When they reached the tree, the heat from the flames kept them back at a safe distance, but the view was tremendous.

Arty said, "Frrrrrap!"

Jan replied, "I will miss you too, Arty. Oh my goodness!" she said. "I understood what you said!"

"Yes," said Ouch. "When you become a true friend of a bookworm, you begin to understand what they are saying."

Jan and Arty embraced, then she looked over at Ouch. He was walking right up to the Fire-Tree. The heat did not seem to bother him as he approached the burning mass of yellow and orange-tipped flames. After all, she reminded herself, he was a dragon.

"What do you have to do, Ouch?" Jan asked after him.

She watched as Ouch broke a small branch off the tree. He returned to Jan with the branch still burning in his hand. "Before the fire goes out," he said, "I will have to make my wish. Are you ready, Jan?"

Leaving such special and unique characters tugged at Jan's heartstrings. She took a deep breath to compose herself, kissed each of her friends on the cheek and said she was ready.

Ouch closed his eyes and made his wish.

Jan started to feel funny, like she was falling into a deep sleep. She shouted into the air as she fell backwards. "I will never forget you all. Thanks for everythingggggggggggggg....."

CHAPTER SEVEN

It wasn't a dream!

"Are you all right, Jan?"

Jan opened her eyes and found herself looking once more into the face of the Janitor. Realising she was on the floor of the janitor's closet, she began to sit up.

"I saw those horrible girls push you in my closet and lock the door. You must have tripped over this bucket or something. Are you all right?" he asked again.

"Yes," Jan told him. "But I was gone for the whole day. How could you have just seen Camilla and Sheila push me in here?"

The janitor frowned with concern. "I think you may have bumped your head, Jan."

"Yes. Maybe," she said. "I just want to go home now."

He helped Jan to her feet and told her he would go back to her classroom and explain everything to Miss Take. He closed the door behind them and as they walked away, Jan turned around to look at the closet door. She smiled to herself. "What a dream," she thought as they carried on. "I can't wait to get home and share it with Granma! It's just like the things she told me she dreamt about in her coma!"

Nearly nine months had passed since Jan's amazing adventure in the janitor's closet. She had told Granma all about it as soon as she got home, and Granma agreed that it sounded just like the dreams that she'd had. Jan often went to share her memories with Granma and these were very special times. They compared notes about the different creatures they had encountered and laughed when Granma remarked that the dragon she had met could have been Ouch's Granpa!

Things had improved a lot at school, and Jan actually began to look forward to going to class each day. Camilla Pitts and her gang no longer bothered with Jan and her friends. They were too frightened to.

Jan had gone to all the children in the playground, one by one, and between them they had documented a list of things that Camilla and the other bullies had done to them.

Then one day, after the dinner break, Jan went over to Camilla and showed her the list. Camilla looked totally stunned! Jan told Camilla that if she ever hurt or upset anyone in the school again, everybody would use their 'BIG-JOINED-TOGETHER-VOICE' and shout to the world, **"Camilla Pitts is a big bully!"**

And if that were not enough, Jan would give the list to the Head Teacher to show Camilla's parents. Camilla always behaved well at home and led her parents to believe that she was a 'perfect little angel'. She realised that her image would be blown if Mummy and Daddy saw the list, and that her state of the art gadgets and her designer wardrobe from all over the world would be confiscated as a punishment. The thought of losing all her precious possessions was too much for her; she started to turn over a new leaf and her days of terrorising people finally came to an end. She would never say "boo!" to anyone again!

Without the distraction of being bullied and frightened all the time, Jan could finally concentrate in class. She didn't have to hide in her imagination and her daydreams anymore! Her class work improved, and her teacher began issuing her with achiever awards right, left and centre.

Miss Take had introduced 'Golden-Time' at the end of the day, which could be used by the children to have a private moment with her to cover any worries that they may have – such as bullying! It really helped to know that the teacher had finally realised who the trouble makers were and that everyone else might need a little bit of help every now and then.

One frosty morning at school, Miss Take asked Jan to take the register along to the secretary. Jan skipped off along the corridor, as happy as anything. She handed in the register and was about to return to class when she realised she was outside the janitor's closet. Jan stopped for a moment outside the door and smiled as she remembered her dream. Then she walked on.

"Pssssssssssssst!"

'Who said that?' thought Jan. She looked behind her. "Oh my heart!" yelped Jan.

The door had opened just a crack, and Jan had seen Ouch peeping through!

"Pssssssssssst! Jan, come here!" The red dragon beckoned to Jan to come over to him.

Suddenly the school secretary walked out of her room. "Is something wrong, Jan? Did you forget something?"

"Eh, no," said Jan, and she turned to go back to her classroom.

"Hold on, Jan. You've dropped a piece of paper." The secretary picked it up and handed it to Jan. "Off you go now. Back to your class."

As she turned away, a puzzled Jan unfurled the paper, which had a message scribbled on it. She began to read the note as she strolled slowly on.

Dear Jan,

After you left, chaos hit us all and the biggest nightmare occurred.

My mum's new eggs have been stolen by evil little snotlings and Rain-bow has disappeared on her way to Unicorn Island!

Please HELP!

Come back to the closet as soon as you can.

Love Ouch.

xxx

PART II

CHAPTER EIGHT

The worst pain ever!

Ouch watched anxiously through the crack in the closet door as Jan read the note, praying that she would come and help him again. However, Jan seemed rooted to the spot. She was hesitating in the corridor, clearly torn between investigating the closet and returning to class, behaving as expected and maintaining her new, trouble-free existence.

"Pssssssssssst! Jan, come here!" The young dragon beckoned to Jan again from behind the closet door.

It wasn't a dream after all! "Oh my goodness," thought Jan as she stood mesmerised, staring at the door. Tall, red and scaly with big blue eyes and a pouting bottom lip, Ouch the dragon looked miserable and in need of Jan's help.

But the school secretary was getting annoyed. "Well, off you go!"

Jan turned reluctantly to go back to her classroom. She shot a quick look at the door, but Ouch had closed it.

The secretary, turning to go back into her office, paused and sniffed the air. "Jan, can you smell smoke?" she asked. Jan shook her head. "Oh well, must be burnt sausages again for dinner," the secretary remarked, adjusting her spectacles. "Off you go now, back to your class."

Still bewildered and confused at coming face to face with a character from her dream in her own world, Jan walked slowly to the double doors at the end of the corridor. Keeping her eyes peeled to make sure that the secretary had returned to her office, she hid out of sight behind the doors, smoothed out the crumpled piece of paper and read it over and over.

Excitement ran through Jan as she read it and realised that her adventure must have actually happened. She just *had* to go back and help Ouch and Rain-bow, but how would she get back to the janitor's closet without anyone catching her? She would just have to chance returning. This was too important.

She waited behind the double doors until the secretary had disappeared behind her office door, then tiptoed towards the closet. However, as she approached the door, the secretary came out of her room again with a strange look on her face. She looked thin-lipped and grave. Startled, Jan froze.

"Oh! You're still here. Come into my office please Jan." Oh no. Now she was for it. But what did she want? Surely Jan couldn't be in trouble for just standing in the corridor, could she? And she looked so odd!

Jan looked back at the closet door. Ouch's red dragon face was looking through the crack in the door and his big blue eyes were begging her to come to him. Jan shook her head and shrugged helplessly.

In the busy school office, the secretary took Jan into a quiet corner and nodded towards some seats. This was all very strange and Jan wondered what on earth was going on. The secretary explained that she had just had just a phone call from Jan's parents and that her mum was coming to collect her. She stepped towards Jan and, tilting her head to one side and still looking very solemn, she gave Jan a kind of reassuring pat on the arm. "Have a seat here dear, beside me. Your mum won't be long." Jan found this very unsettling and was beginning to wonder if she should be stressed right now.

Five minutes later, her mum arrived and Jan, still wondering why she was there, saw that there was something definitely wrong with her mum. Her eyes were all red and puffy; she looked terrible.

Jan's mum thanked the ladies in the office and ushered her out to the car park.

"Have you been crying, Mum?" Jan's mum didn't respond.

"Mum, what's wrong? Why have you come for me?" Again, Jan's mum stayed silent.

As they got into the car, Jan's unsettled feeling began to turn to panic and she said louder and more urgently, "Mum!"

"Jan, just wait until we get home!" her mum snapped at her tensely. Now Jan was really worried. What could be wrong?

As they approached their home, Jan realised that something just dreadful must have happened; she was feeling sick with nerves by the time the car came to a stop outside their little cottage. Jan watched her mum wipe her eyes as she followed her into the living room. Her dad and her brother were both already there. Now Jan knew it was really bad if her dad was off work and her brother was not at college.

"Sit down Jan," her mum told her. Jan sat down facing her dad and her brother. They looked at each other in silence for a few moments; her mum seemed to be struggling to find words to say and fighting to hold back tears. Suddenly, the awful truth came to Jan in a flash.

"Granma, Granma!" Jan screamed for her all the way up the stairs as she ran to her grandmother's bedroom.

Jan was followed up the stairs by her family. She could hear them telling her to slow down and just wait until they could talk to her.

Jan stopped and stared through the open door, hardly able to bring herself to go in. Finally she pulled herself together and forced herself over the threshold. Looking around the room she muttered, almost to herself, "Where is my Granma?" But the little girl didn't need to be told. In her heart, she knew what had happened.

The room felt cold, empty and lifeless. Granma was gone.

Jan's mum put her arms around her shoulders. Jan pushed them away roughly and went over to Granma's bed. She sat down and hugged the pretty pink embroidered pillow fiercely to her chest. Tears were streaming down her face and her breath came in great shuddering sobs. She looked at her mum, then her brother. They were both crying too.

Jan's dad moved closer and sat beside her. "Your grandmother was old, Jan. You know she wasn't well." The words seemed very hard for her dad to say; his voice was shaky and she could feel his hands trembling as he tried to hold her hand. Jan threw her father's hand away and stood up.

"But where is my Granma? What have you done with her?" Jan demanded. She knew what had happened and that her questions were pointless, but she didn't want to believe it. Her heart was pounding and she had never felt so much pain in her whole life.

"Calm down Jan, please." Jan's mum tried to comfort her. "We need to talk about this." But Jan's mum could not say anything that would take away the grief that was ripping through her heart.

Her parents tried to explain but the words were like an echo in Jan's head, going round and round till she was left with a meaningless wall of sound.

Unable to stand it any longer, Jan ran out of the bedroom and down the stairs, through the kitchen and out the back door. She had to get away, out of the house and away from the pain. Her parents ran after her but Jan was too quick. She tore through the back garden and sped away from the house as fast as she could.

Eventually, Jan slowed down and came to a halt. She was out of breath and panting hard. The pain in her body from running and the pain in her heart from losing Granma were tearing her apart and would not go away. Tears poured uncontrollably down Jan's cheeks, and her body shook with shock and anguish.

It felt like this went on for hours, then finally she looked up. Wiping her eyes, she saw her school through the trees. Somehow this set the tears flowing again. Jan had told Granma all about how she had finally coped with her bullying classmates, and how well she was doing at school now. Granma often used to tell Jan how proud she was of her and always encouraged her with whatever she was doing.

Why, why, did she have to die? Jan could not imagine her life without Granma. She loved her so much, and on top of everything else she was the only one who really understood Jan's daydreams. She hadn't ever really told anyone else about them, but she and Granma had discussed them often.

Jan had never known anyone that had died before and she just could not understand it. The young girl was exhausted and nothing in the world made any sense to her any more.

She sat on a log and watched the children at her school run around the playground. Unexpectedly, Jan drifted into one of her "*weirdest of time*" daydreams.

In her mind she could see herself going to school carrying a big black case. The other children asked if it was a violin she was holding but she told them it wasn't and unzipped the case, taking out a huge hammer! Raising the enormous tool of destruction, she gave her school tormentors just enough time to scarper and dive down the large holes that had mysteriously appeared in the ground before beginning the mass obliteration. After all of the children had disappeared down their holes to safety, Jan would wait patiently for a head to pop up. One by one, curiosity got the better of the little terrors and they would poke their heads slowly up above ground level. Then Jan would act in a flash, smashing them back down the hole with a hefty blow of the hammer. It was just like the game she had played with Granma last summer at the town carnival.

Jan realised she was venting her anger at the wrong people. "Thing is," Jan thought, "who is there to be angry at? Who is to blame for taking Granma away from me?"

Thinking about Granma made her snap out of her trance. Nobody was to blame for this; as her dad had said, Granma was old and wasn't well. Things like this just happened, and, hard as it was, no amount of daydreaming could make Jan forget and no amount of wishing would bring her back. What was she thinking of?

Then suddenly, an idea sprang into her head. Ouch the dragon had told her that he had made a wish at the magical Fire-Tree for someone to come into his world and help him with the school bully. The wish had come true and Jan had been sent to assist.

That was it! Jan would go back to the janitor's closet, find Ouch and ask him to make a wish at the Fire-Tree for her. Jan would ask him to wish that Granma had not died!

CHAPTER NINE

Back to the land of Zoogly

Jan tried to creep unnoticed through the crowd of children getting ready to line up. She had nearly made it to the doors when a familiar voice shouted, "Jan!" It was Lucy, one of Jan's best friends. Lucy was glad to see her friend and came rushing over.

"I thought you were sent home? Miss Take told us that you weren't feeling well and you went home."

It was true in a way; Jan really didn't feel well but it was a different kind of pain to any she'd had before. She heaved an enormous sigh and looked down at the ground. She just couldn't tell her friend what had happened because she would simply burst with tears. Her bronze curls fell across her face and she brushed the dampness from her swollen eyes, but she was determined not to cry any more. She had to be strong, get into school and reach the janitor's closet. Jan set her jaw, brought her head up swiftly and said, "I'm fine now Lucy, so let's get to class."

As Jan walked into school, Camilla Pitts pushed past the other children to get to her. "Oh, Jan you're back, how wonderful. We all missed you. Are you feeling better?"

Jan knew Camilla didn't really care about her. After all, it wasn't that long ago that she was the reason Jan hated even going to school. Although it was good that Camilla had stopped bullying and was trying to change, Jan just couldn't deal with her now. Her mind was on an important mission, and that was to get to the closet no matter what! So she turned and just walked away.

"Where are you going, Jan?" Camilla shouted after her.

But Jan could not care about anyone else at the moment.

Lucy cried after her. "You're going the wrong way. Come back Jan, we'll be late for class!"

Jan looked back at her friend and, beginning visibly to shake again, she said, "Tell Miss Take that I'm not feeling well after all and I decided to go home!"

Lucy saw that her friend was shaking and suddenly pale; she really didn't look well. She agreed to let Miss Take know. Grateful that her friend hadn't pressed the issue further, Jan went into the girl's rest room and waited until everyone had gone into their classrooms; she could hear the hubbub dying away as doors closed and the corridors became quiet and empty once more. However, empty corridors meant that she couldn't hide in a crowd and she'd be easily spotted. She wondered how she would get to the janitor's closet without being noticed.

All the staff at the school must have been told about Granma passing away, so how would she explain things if she got caught? Thinking for a moment, Jan developed an idea. She pulled her jacket hood over her head and tucked in her long hair, pulling the cords tight. She grabbed a handful of paper towels from beside one of the sinks and slowly opened the door. Someone was passing; she closed it quickly, praying that she hadn't been seen. Listening carefully, she opened the door again. It was clear, so off she went, desperate to get to the closet.

Up the stairs, through the double doors, across the corridor towards the main door and then she would be there.

She reached the top of the stairs without incident, but just then the janitor turned the corner and pushed the door open to discover her standing at the top step.

"What are you doing out of your class?" he asked. "Where are you going?"

Jan had pushed all the paper towels up to hide her face as soon as she saw him. "By dose is bleeding and I hab to hurry to de durse!" Jan said, trying to sound like her nose was blocked with blood. She hated telling fibs, but just now she had no option. She just *had* to get to the closet!

"Well hurry up child, before I have to clean up your blood!" The janitor held the door open and she rushed through. Jan risked a look back and sighed with relief; he had gone down the stairs and out of sight.

Ahead, it was clear both ways so she ran over and opened the closet door. Hesitating for a moment and wondering if she were doing the right thing, she thought about Granma. Her resolve hardened, she went in and closed the door behind her.

The first time she had been in the closet she had been terrified; scared of the dark and of small spaces it had been a nightmare to be locked in the closet. She was different now though; stronger and unafraid. And she was here for a different reason.

Everything was dark and silent. Her heart was beating fast and the sound of her own breathing seemed extraordinarily loud. But nothing was happening! Where was Ouch? Had he gone? The closet was so small, surely if he were still here she would be able to feel him? And where were all the colourful swirls and the feeling of falling through space that she had experienced the last time she'd been in the closet? Jan dreaded the thought that Ouch had left without her.

Moments that seemed like hours passed and still nothing happened. Jan was aware that it was now getting very warm in the closet and it suddenly seemed more full of stuff than she had remembered. Starting to feel claustrophobic and hemmed in again, her breathing got deeper and faster as her despair increased, and it was making a terrible noise. Her sharp intakes of breath were making a horrible, loud, grating sound. Jan forced herself to hold her breath for a moment, to quiet things down and get a grip on herself, but the noise continued. Suddenly, she realised why it felt like there was less space in the closet; the noise was not coming from her at all and, worse than that, she was not alone!

Suddenly someone tapped her on the shoulder and she nearly jumped out of her skin. Then, a whispering voice said, "Why are we standing so still, Jan?"

"Ahhhh!" Jan screamed and turned round. In the darkness, she could just make out the outline of a familiar shape.

"Oh, thank goodness, Ouch, it's you!" Jan gave her dragon friend the biggest hug and then, still holding on, she began to cry.

"She's gone Ouch, my Granma is gone!"

Ouch, shocked by Jan's unexpected revelation, held his crying friend and leaned down to whisper in her ear.

"Looks like we have a lot to tell each other. Let's go to my house."

And with that, Jan began to feel the familiar sense of falling through space that she had experienced before. She closed her eyes as they spiralled into a whirlwind of colour, falling deeper and deeper. They held on tightly to each other and gradually, everything became lighter.

Jan opened her eyes and realised she was being safely cradled in her friend's small but very strong arms. She felt tiny but protected and for a split second, being held like this almost made her forget the tormenting pain.

Ouch very tenderly wiped a tear away from her eye and held her for a few moments longer.

"I'm all right now. Thank you Ouch." Jan jumped out of his arms and on to the ground. Ouch watched as Jan looked around at the trees, sniffling and sighing deeply.

A familiar warm wind blew around the two of them and many unspoken moments passed. Ouch watched his little pal, who looked lost and troubled, with great concern. She began to move a stone around with her foot and his heart wrenched as he realised this fragile little human seemed to be carrying an almighty hurt within her. "Are you ready to go to my house, Jan?"

Jan collected herself with some difficulty and looked up into his very kind face, "Yes, I'm ready now. Where do you live Ouch?"

"Number 17 Snuggery Cove." He said proudly, "It's not far from here but perhaps we should fly. I know how you like to fly, Jan." Ouch gave Jan a big smile and she returned it, knowing that her friend was trying his very best to make her feel better.

"Up you go!" The young dragon lay down to let Jan climb on to his back. Off they went, high into the sky. Jan saw again the view that she would never, ever forget; the city of Zoogly.

Castles, mountains, forests and lakes stretched out before them. Jan shook her head in astonishment as she remembered that all of this was riding on the back of beautiful butterfly that was suspended in time and space in the great universe. This awesome planet was surrounded by other magnificent worlds and glittering stars that twinkled their magic beside them.

The last time Jan had seen this she could not believe it and the same nervous exhilaration ran through her as she marvelled at the sights. But this time, she was here for a more important reason than to fight off the school bully; this time, she had a very important wish to make!

CHAPTER TEN

Meet the family

Ouch landed slowly and cautiously, taking great care of his friend. Jan looked around and saw many arched entrances to caves that were dotted all over the side of a rocky hill.

"That's my cave up there," Ouch said as he pointed up the hill. "Number 17, next to where that wolf is standing."

Spotting them, the big white wolf came bounding down the hill in what seemed like enormous strides, almost like he was flying.

"I hope that wolf is friendly!" asked Jan.

"Oh yes. That's Seezer; he lives with his family next door to us," Ouch told her as he helped Jan to the ground.

The wolf started laughing as he came up to Ouch. Smirking and extremely cocky, the furry canine said, "I'm coming with you Ouch. I told you I would get to, so in your face!"

"No way!" said Ouch, shaking his head.

The wolf pranced around the dragon. "Don't fight it, just go with the flow blazer breath!" Seezer the wolf grinned as he began to scratch his ear casually with his back leg.

He studied Jan from head to toe with his big emerald green eyes, so striking against his snow white fur. Jan was more than a little nervous of the wolf but he seemed friendly enough so she gave him a wary smile.

Ouch began to stomp up the hill. "We'll see about that!" he cried over his shoulder to the wolf. The dragon didn't seem happy at all and he stumbled clumsily, falling over in his upward haste. Jan remembered that his large feet had caused him problems more than once on her last visit. His loss of balance reduced the argumentative young wolf to fits of laughter as he said, "Go for it my friend, but our mothers agreed on it while you were away."

The long-haired animal, half the size of Jan, watched Ouch go before turning his attention to her. "So, the last time you were here little girl, you tamed the fuzzbutt monster. But do you really think you and that stupid flame thrower can find the thieves, all by yourselves?" Seezer narrowed his eyes and waited for an answer.

"I don't know what you mean," Jan replied.

From half way up the hill Ouch shouted, "Jan, just ignore him, he has the mental age of a three-year-old. Come up and meet my mum."

Jan did not hesitate and took off up the hill after him.

Seezer watched as Jan ran to the dragon. Then the wolf closed his beautiful green eyes and a third, hidden, eye on his forehead opened. It was the colour of deep burning amber and it followed Jan as she moved quickly up the hill.

Seezer could read the feelings of others with his magical third eye, but it only worked if his other two eyes were closed. He had five other brothers and sisters in his pack, but this was a rare gift and he was the only one that had been born with this incredible intuition.

Then, as fast as it opened, the fur eyelid closed, hiding his golden stare. Slowly, he opened his other two eyes and tilted his head to one side. Seezer had felt the pain of Jan's loss for her grandmother as if it had ripped through his own heart as well as Jan's. Unable to contain these feelings, the wolf pointed his head to the sky and howled in sympathy for Jan's heartache.

Jan arrived at the top of the hill and heard the most piercing howl to ever reach her ears. It went through her heart like a knife, but at the same time she felt strangely comforted. She looked back down at the wolf in amazement.

The young girl and the young wolf's eyes connected and suddenly she felt a peculiar understanding of the animal, a closeness that she could not explain.

Ouch tugged at Jan's hand, breaking the spell. "Come on Jan, this way. My mum can't wait to meet you."

Jan glanced back at the wolf once more, wondering about the strange kinship she suddenly felt for him, before following Ouch into the cave. She was surprised at how homely it was. There were large seats with cushions and a table with a clay pot that held beautiful flowers. Four other tunnels led off from this comfortable area and Jan assumed they must lead to other rooms. A large dragon that could only be Ouch's mum walked through an arch to greet them. She was a big reddish pink dragon with blue eyes and long black eyelashes, just like her son. She was wearing a flower behind her ear and was carrying a tray with drinks and cakes on it. She saw Jan and yelped with joy.

"You must be Jan, come give me a hug! I have heard so much about you. Thank you, thank you for coming to help!" The loving dragon put down her tray on the table and picked Jan up, kissing her face all over. Jan was a little unnerved by this. She remembered that Ouch had got his name because when he hatched, his mum had been so excited that she had accidentally blown a flame into his face and singed his eyelashes. Jan hoped fervently that she was more in control of herself now!

40

"My name is Bloom. Ouch's father is called Brick, but he is not here just now." All of a sudden, the mood of the cheerful mother dragon changed. Her voice faltered; she looked troubled and began to cry as she sat down.

"Don't cry, Mum," Ouch said as he knelt down and held his mum's hand. "You know it will start me off and I won't be able to stop."

Jan watched as both mother and son rocked back and forth, crying and wailing, comforting each other.

'Good grief,' thought Jan. 'What a bizarre sight! I wonder if that's what I looked like when I was crying about Granma?'

"What's wrong?" she asked aloud.

Ouch and his mum told Jan that two days ago, their three baby dragon eggs were stolen in the middle of the night. Ouch's mum was devastated and Ouch's dad had gone out looking for the thieves, but he had not come back yet.

"Who do you think stole them?" Jan enquired.

A rough voice behind her said, "It was the evil little snotlings who live in Fairy Forest!"

Jan turned around to find Seezer sitting in the entrance of the cave.

"Come in Seezer." Ouch's mum welcomed the wolf in to her home.

Bloom stood up and told her son that Seezer would be going with him and Jan to find his father and the stolen eggs, even if Ouch didn't want him to go.

"Seezer will help protect you," she said. Turning to Jan, she exclaimed, "Honestly, they're so competitive! They squabble all of the time, just like brothers."

She also explained to Jan that the best way to get to Fairy Forest would be for her son to carry Jan on his back and for Seezer, with his incredible speed, to cover the ground below.

"Now before you set off for Fairy Forest, I want you all to eat up and I will go and pack some food for the journey." The kind lady dragon handed the tray of cakes and drinks to Jan and went back through the cave. Jan looked at the colourful cakes but she wasn't hungry.

She found it incredible that Ouch's mother would let them go off on such a dangerous mission themselves, especially when Ouch's dad hadn't come back. She said this to Ouch, who explained that his mum said they had proved themselves by dealing with the fuzzbutt monster and that she felt they would be safe together. "After all," Ouch said with rolling eyes, "Mum says that you were a saviour sent to save her son the last time, so she prayed for you to rescue her other hatchlings this time. So we just can't let her down, can we? Besides that," Ouch straightened up and tilted his chin upwards, "I need to prove myself. I wasn't exactly the bravest of dragons on your last visit, was I?"

Jan looked at Ouch compassionately and said, "OK, OK. But what about Rain-bow? Your note said that she had disappeared! And where is Arty? It sounds like we could really use his help too."

Ouch looked at Seezer and then back to Jan. "Arty has gone back to his home for the summer holidays. Rain-bow went to visit her family, but she was supposed to be back here over a week ago!"

Ouch told Jan that, after Jan had returned to her own world and left Zoogly, Rain-bow's unicorn horn had begun to grow. It hadn't happened before because she had to complete a special good deed in order for it to happen and by helping Jan with the bullies, she had fulfilled that. The horn grew beautifully.

The unicorn was so happy that she finally had her horn, but she was dreadfully disappointed that Jan couldn't be there to see it. The magical pony, who had been going to stay with Ouch for the holidays, had decided to pay a surprise visit to her parents so that they could see the transformation, have her party on Unicorn Island and return to spend the rest of her summer vacation with Ouch and his family. But, as Ouch said, she had been due back over a week ago and everyone was worried.

Jan was upset for all of the problems that were facing her friends, but it also reminded her of her own sadness. Overwhelmed, her eyes began to fill with tears. Jan moved closer to Ouch and put her hands up to his face. "Dear friend," she said, "please don't be angry with me, but before I can help you, I need you to do something for me first."

Ouch looked confused for a moment, then remembering what Jan had said in the closet he said, "Is it about your grandmother, Jan?"

"Yes. I need you to make a wish at the Fire-Tree and make Granma alive again, PLEASE Ouch!"

Ouch looked at Seezer in dismay and then he put his little hands over his face.

Seezer put a comforting paw on to the dragon's leg and gave out a little supportive whimper of compassion. Ouch took a deep breath and looked at Jan.

"I am so sorry Jan; the Fire-Tree won't grant wishes to bring life back from the other side."

Jan looked shocked. "What do you mean?" she cried. "You told me it was magic! It helped you. Why won't it help me?"

But the dragon put his head in his hands again. Jan buried her head in one of the cushions on the seat she was sitting on and began to cry.

"You see," said Seezer, "when any of our family die, they go over to the "Kingdom" and we are not sad because we know they are happy there."

Jan looked up, bewildered, and shook her head. She didn't understand. Ouch put his hand on Jan's head and stroked her long red hair. He described to Jan how wonderful the Kingdom was. It was a place of great joy where all the old and departed creatures went after life had ended for them. Those living on rejoiced, remembered and talked all the time about their loved ones who had moved on.

Bloom had returned unseen by anyone and had been standing listening quietly in the corner of the cave; she spoke and her soft voice made Jan jump.

"There is something you can do, Jan," she said. "If you get to Unicorn Island, you can ask to see the King of the Unicorns. He has a magic mirror; if you ask him very nicely he may allow you to use it."

"What does it do?" asked Jan, her eyes wide.

"Amongst other things, it allows people to see their loved ones on the other side. You would be able to see your grandmother again!"

CHAPTER ELEVEN

Journey to Fairy Forest

Jan, Ouch and Seezer had made their final preparations for their journey. They said their goodbyes and set off for Fairy Forest. To begin with, all three walked out of the city to a wave of friendly well-wishers, who gave advice on how to deal with the evil little snotlings who lived in the forest.

An old dragon advised staying well clear of the snotlings, as their green slimy skin was poisonous and their red bulging eyes could put an unexpected traveller in a trance. Another suggested that Ouch should fly over their heads and drop boulders, squashing the little critters to a pulp. Snotlings were small, about the size of a human baby, and they could dart very quickly about the forest, hiding in the undergrowth and jumping out of trees. Although they had little wings folded on their backs, they only helped with gliding through the air. They had lost the use of them for proper flying long ago because they spent most of their time scavenging on the forest floor, looking for injured or helpless creatures. Their faces were flat, as if they had been trapped in the fridge door, and they had large mouths that oozed black tar from between their teeth. Their daily hunt across the swamp was a speciality and they would cover their victims with swamp spit, leave them to harden and return every seven days at feeding time!

The urge for Jan to see Granma in the magic mirror was overwhelming, but she didn't like the sound of all of this and she was beginning to wonder what she was getting herself into. What if these evil snotling things harmed her and she couldn't get back to her mum and dad?

"What are you thinking about, Jan?" Ouch asked.

"To tell you the truth, I'm a bit worried about these nasty green things that everyone's been warning us about. Mum and Dad have enough to worry about without losing me too!"

Seezer stopped in front of them. "You don't think I would let them get you, do you Jan? That's what I'm here for, to protect you."

Ouch also turned to face her. "And me too Jan. I would never, ever let anything happen to you."

Jan was touched by the reassurance her protective friends were giving her. She was beginning to feel whole again and a glimmer of hope and excitement flashed through her as she realised that a kind of healing was taking place. It felt good and the pressure of the day was beginning to drain away. Surrounding herself with friends and keeping busy was just the medicine she needed.

"I'm hungry," she said, suddenly aware that her appetite had returned as her mood had lightened. "Let's see what your mum has packed for us to eat, shall we?" And with that, the three friends sat down to picnic, devouring the scrumptious food and not leaving a crumb.

The blue and red sun was setting, but it was still warm. Jan asked Ouch and Seezer about the warm breeze that always seemed to be around.

"We're fortunate here with our warm wind; it blows day and night," Ouch explained. "It comes from the butterfly's wings. On top of that, Zoogly's sun only ever half sets here; it just dips below the horizon and no more. That means it never really gets cold, and it never gets totally dark either, not like some planets that don't have any daylight. Isn't it nice where you live Jan?"

Jan laughed. "We have some nice warm weather but it mainly rains where I come from." Ouch and Seezer stared at her uncomprehendingly. "You know, like water falling from the sky." She waited for them to understand but they still looked puzzled.

"You mean a giant cries and his teardrops hit your planet?" asked Seezer, doubtfully. He looked at Ouch but he shrugged his shoulders, none the wiser.

Jan giggled. "I suppose you could look at it like that. You are so funny." She reached out to stroke Seezer on the head, but the wolf jumped back in surprise.

"What's wrong?" asked Jan. "I only wanted to pat you."

"What for?" he asked. Then he said, "No don't tell me, I will feel why." Seezer closed his eyes and his third, magic, eye opened up.

Jan's jaw dropped as she stared in astonishment at the beautiful golden brown eye.

"What on earth...?" Jan's eyes widened as she turned to Ouch and the dragon smiled back at her. Ouch explained to her about Seezer's rare gift. "Wow!" exclaimed Jan.

Seezer closed the one eye on his forehead and gradually widened his other emerald green eyes. "Ah, I see now," he said. "You want to make yourself feel better by stroking my fur. Do you humans do that a lot in your world?"

Jan considered this; she had never thought about stroking an animal like that before. "I suppose we do. I used to have a dog, which is kind of like a wolf, but he only had two eyes. He had curly hair that I loved to feel and brush and yes, it did make me feel better. He liked it too though."

"All right, let's try it." He walked over to Jan and lay down beside her on the grass.

Jan cuddled him and stroked behind his ears. Suddenly, his back leg started to twitch and he rolled around on to his back. He seemed to like this and nuzzled her arm as she rubbed his tummy.

Ouch looked over in disgust and decided he could watch the sickening display no longer. He stood up and because he had stuffed his belly too much, he gave out a loud thunderous burp, making Jan jump.

"When you two are ready we should get going!" Ouch clearly looked upset and he kicked over the picnic basket, on purpose!

Jan was taken by surprise and wondered what was wrong with Ouch. Then it came to her quickly. He was jealous! She ran over to him and hugged him.

"What's that for?" the dragon asked.

Jan smiled up at him. "For being a big silly lump of course."

"I'm not a silly ahhhhhh…." Ouch fell backwards over the basket, arms stretched out grabbing at the air as he bounced once, then twice. He rolled on the ground and quickly coming to a stop, he pulled himself together as if nothing comical had just happened. He shot a glance to the others and said, "I'm fine, perfectly fine. Nothing to see here."

There was silence for a moment, then, all three held their tummies and wailed with laughter, breaking the tension and uniting the friends again.

With the picnic area cleared up, the three resumed their journey, but this time Ouch and Jan took to the air and Seezer sped like a lightning bolt across the earth. Jan was amazed at the speed of the wolf and could barely make out his shape as he kept up with the dragon's flight above him. She held on tight to her friend's neck and marvelled at the shadow his great form was creating on the earth, disappearing now and then between the hills.

Ouch looked over his shoulder and shouted to Jan. "We're nearing the edge of Fairy Forest. Are you ready to land?"

She looked ahead and saw the beginnings of a large tree-covered area. "Yes, let's go down."

Ouch began to circle and slowly came down to earth, grabbing the ground with his big feet and running a few steps. He lay down and allowed Jan to slide off his back.

Out of nowhere, Seezer approached. Panting he said, "I don't like the looks of things in that forest. I can feel hatred and evil all around us. We had better be careful!"

CHAPTER TWELVE

Snotling new-leader feast!

Zoogly's blue and red sun had finally dipped behind the hills, reducing the light to twilight; however the three friends could still see quite clearly as they approached the trees. It was darker in the forest though; stepping over branches and fallen logs as they entered, they looked up to see the remains of the light stabbing through the tops of the very tall trees.

"I can't wait to see a fairy," Jan said excitedly.

Seezer huffed and shook an acorn from his fur. "You're more likely to see an evil little snotling before a fairy. Fairies hardly ever appear in front of you."

"I've seen a fairy," said Ouch.

"When?" demanded Seezer, screwing up his nose in disbelief.

"On our way back from Star Lake after our holidays last year. My family were all tired from flying so we landed outside Fairy Forest. Not this side, the other one. That's when I saw a fairy splashing over a pond. It was so beautiful."

"No way! I bet you're making that up, because fairies don't like water…" But just then, a rustling noise in the undergrowth a little way off made the wolf stop what he was saying. "Shhhhhh! I feel something is close by."

From deeper in the forest, a strange groaning sound could be heard, faint at first but getting louder as the three moved carefully towards it. A large mound of disgusting, sticky-looking glop sat piled high in the middle of a clearing. Green moss had grown over it and it looked very solid.

The three friends stopped in the trees at the edge of the clearing until they determined that it was safe to approach the mound. Seezer sniffed the air and told the others to stay back. Venturing closer and stopping just beside the mound, he closed his green eyes and with his magic third eye open, he concentrated.

"Yes!" The wolf sprang up and began to jump around excitedly. "You'll never believe who is trapped in this spit-ball rock. Guess, go on, guess!"

Ouch and Jan ran over. "Just tell us who it is you annoying fur-ball!" Ouch couldn't take it anymore. He began to pull at the sticky moss-covered hill with his little hands; it crackled and, pulling off chunks, he uncovered a long pointy horn. A familiar voice whinnied to him. "Oh, thank goodness it's you, Ouch. I am so glad to see you! I thought the snotlings were back to eat me."

Jan's head snapped up as she recognised her friend's voice. "Yes, brilliant! It's Rain-bow!"

Ouch and Seezer pulled and tore the rest of the prison apart as fast as they could, setting the little white unicorn free. Rain-bow reared up on her back legs and shook the mess loose from her long flowing mane. Stepping proudly out of the clutter, her amazing gold unicorn horn glimmered as the slices of sunlight shone all around her.

Jan rushed towards her, putting both arms round her neck, hugging tight while the unicorn nuzzled her back.

"I never thought I would see you again Jan. Thank you for rescuing me."

"It wasn't me Rain-bow, it was Seezer who heard and felt you and Ouch organised the search."

The unicorn thanked them all and described her terrible ordeal with the snotlings. Four slimy green creatures had stopped her from getting to Unicorn Island. On her way there from Ouch's house, she had landed to graze at the edge of the forest when they appeared from nowhere, lassoing her with a rope made of moss. She had struggled, reared and kicked but they tied the other end of the rope around a tree and began to pelt her with snotling spit. She was helpless and could do nothing but wait while the spit hardened and became her tomb. The small white filly knew she had a long wait; her parents weren't expecting her because it was to be a surprise visit. Only Ouch knew when she was due back and he had immediately raised the alarm when she was late.

During the happy reunion, Ouch told Rain-bow about the missing dragon eggs and his dad.

"We'd better get moving," he said.

Tired and still anxious, the search continued through the forest for the missing members of the dragon family. They reached a swampy area so Rain-bow carried Jan on her back. Jan had never ridden on a pony before and it was something she had always yearned to do back home. The girl knew she was privileged to be riding on not just a pony, but a magical, magnificent unicorn!

Jan took the opportunity to tell her friend quietly about her terrible loss; Rain-bow was so sorry to hear about Jan's grandmother. Jan was asking about the magic mirror that Ouch's mother had mentioned when Seezer, who had been scouting the way ahead, suddenly came rushing back into view.

"We'll have to be very quiet," the wolf told them. "There's a snotling camp ahead! You all stay here and I'll get close enough to feel and hear what's going on."

They watched him disappear through the bushes anxiously.

"Here's a nice soft area," Ouch said. "Let's snuggle up behind this fallen tree."

As they made themselves comfortable, Jan asked Rain-bow about the Unicorn King. "Do you think he will let me see Granma through the magic mirror?"

"He will if I ask him." The little unicorn looked confident and batted her long eyelashes.

"Do you really think so? Why are you so sure?" Jan asked.

"Because he's my father, and anyway, if he says no, my mum will make him. He always does anything she asks!"

Jan and Rain-bow gave each other a knowing look and hugged as only good supportive friends could.

50

Just then, Seezer came bounding back. He panted for a few seconds then circled and sat facing them.

"There's good news and bad news. What do you want first?"

Ouch shook his head. "Why do you always do this, just tell us for fuzzbutt sake!"

"All right, calm down before you bust into flames. Good news is, all three eggs are safe, bad news is, they're going to make an omelette tonight in honour of the new-leader feast!"

"What!" Ouch leapt up and snorted out a flame, sizzling a branch above him, which promptly fell on his head.

"Ouch!" said Ouch. "But that's terrible!" Turning to go deeper into the forest, he said, "I can't let that happen. I have to save them right now!"

With one leap, Seezer jumped in front of the dragon and blocked his path. "No, you can't just go rushing in like that! It would be suicide. However, I have a plan."

The wolf explained all about the new-leader feast. Every five years, a new snotling leader was crowned. Seezer had stayed close to the camp long enough to hear the three snotlings who were up for nomination bragging and taking it in turn to describe their brave deeds to the other snotlings, who were assembled around a fire. The first candidate told how he had stolen three dragon eggs and scared away the father dragon. This was considered a great feat, but the second candidate had astonished the gathering with claims of catching a fairy. He had imprisoned the fairy within a waterfall and contained her in a jar that he had held up for all to see. Loud cheers followed this display and it looked like candidate number two had won. It was well known that to catch a fairy of the woods was well-nigh impossible and only by surrounding the fairy in water could the snotling be sure she wouldn't be able to turn him into a beetle – or something worse! This would be difficult to beat as it showed not only immense bravery but brains as well. However, a smug little snotling had then stood up and, pausing dramatically for a few seconds, had announced, "I have caught a magnificent unicorn."

His announcement commanded a stunned silence.

With a big smile he looked around, meeting the screwed-up, ugly little faces of the other snotlings, who clearly didn't believe the third candidate's outrageous claims. Catching a flying unicorn with their magical powers and sharp golden horns? It was unheard of! A sudden eruption of laughter straightened the evil little snotling's smile and he stamped his feet furiously. "I *have* caught one, you fools, and I can prove it!" he exclaimed.

His story was confirmed by the three other snotlings who had helped to hold down and spit-ball his find; they had given a green snotling promise to keep the secret until now. The gathering decided that, later that night, they would all go to the imprisoned unicorn and feast on the helpless creature while leadership was handed over to the winner.

Finishing his recounting of the facts, Seezer grinned at Ouch and said, "That, my dear friend, is when we will go into their camp and get your little brothers and sister."

CHAPTER THIRTEEN

The rescue

An hour of munching on apples and raspberries had fortified the four as they began their rescue mission. Ouch once again had eaten too much and burped as they set off.

"You'll need to make sure that's all out of your system before we go much further," Seezer told him as he shared his plan. "We don't want you burping at the wrong moment and letting the snotlings know we're there! We'll go around the outside of the camp and wait until they have all gone."

"But what if they leave someone to guard the eggs?" Jan asked anxiously. She had no wish to end up buried inside a disgusting spit-ball rock, let alone a meal for the evil little creatures!

"I've already thought of that. Ouch, you're going to cause a distraction and make any leftover snotlings chase you while we move in for the rescue."

"Oh and when did you decide this, all by yourself? Who made you the boss of me?" asked Ouch huffily.

"We have no time for this, Ouch. When the snotlings find out there's no unicorn, they'll rush back and make mince-meat out of those eggs! Well not mince-meat exactly, more like quiche but you know what I mean." Seezer gave a nervous little grin.

"Don't you mean an omelette?" Ouch raised his eyebrows and stuck out his tongue.

Jan shook her head and looked at the two in despair. "Come on guys. Don't you two ever agree on anything? This is Ouch's brothers and sister you're joking about!"

Seezer suddenly stiffened. "Hold on!" He sniffed the air and opened his magic eye. "They're coming and they're hungry; everyone hide!"

The friends dived for cover in the thickest undergrowth they could find, getting out of sight not a moment too soon. Twenty or so menacing little voices could be heard passing very close to where they hid. Despite her fear, Jan couldn't resist; she pulled back the branches and carefully moved her head slightly so that she could see the ugly, evil little creatures. She gulped at the shocking sight of their flat, slimy faces and gnarling, sharp teeth.

Pulling her head back into her hiding position, her heart thumping against her ribs, she held her breath and prayed that she hadn't been seen. The noise of the snotlings receded into the distance and everyone heaved a sigh of relief.

"That was close," said Rain-bow.

Seezer leaped out of hiding and began to lead the way. "The camp is just over here, but be very quiet and tread carefully. We don't want to alarm any snotlings left guarding it."

As they approached the camp site, they could see that a small fire was burning and they could just make out the three dragon eggs resting on a bed of leaves. Their worst fears were confirmed as they could see that the eggs were being guarded by two snotlings.

Whispering, the wolf signalled the go-ahead to Ouch to create a diversion.

"What?" Ouch whispered back.

"Make those two snotlings chase you, you idiot!" Seezer hissed, getting rather annoyed.

"What?" The dragon put his hand to his ear and leaned forward. Quite loudly he said, "Sorry, I can't hear you."

The two snotlings' heads snapped up and they peered around to find the source of the noise. Their eyes narrowed as they saw that a rather big and loud dragon was standing a few feet away and he was looking very baffled. A second or two passed as the snotlings stared at Ouch and Seezer, while Seezer, Jan and Rain-bow stared at the snotlings, each frozen in shock. Ouch alone, who was still intent on finding out what Seezer had said, seemed oblivious to the snotlings' presence. Then, all at once, there was pandemonium.

The angry guards had been carrying a large pan to the fire; they dropped it with a loud clang and bolted straight for Ouch. Ouch looked round, startled by the noise, and screamed in surprise as he saw the snotlings bearing down on him. "Ahhhhhh……" He flapped his wings but there was no space; in the close confines of the forest they battered off the trees and branches all around him, keeping him firmly on the ground. Ouch did not want to be caught by the snotlings, poisoned by touching their slimy skin or put in a trance by their red eyes, so he ran as fast as his big clumsy feet would carry him. He attempted to jump over a log, but caught his foot and stumbled, hurtling wildly towards the forest floor.

Frantically twisting his big body round to face the revolting snotlings as he fell, he watched helplessly as they catapulted off the side of a tree and, spreading out their small wings to help them cover the distance to the dragon, headed directly for him.

Smacking hard to the ground on his back, Ouch slammed his head and belched out a huge, long flame. The snotlings, caught in mid-glide above him, were burnt to a crisp in mid air!

Eyes wide in bewilderment, he could not believe the little pieces of charcoaled snotling floating through the breeze blowing towards him. Being peace-loving creatures, it rarely occurred to most dragons to use their fiery breath in this manner and Ouch was no different. Shocked at what he had done, but nevertheless very glad to still be alive, he attempted to sit up.

"Great work dragon!" Seezer leapt on to his friend's tummy, stopping him from getting up. He congratulated him on his triumph and bounced all over, licking the dragon's face.

"Get off, get off you daft wolf." Ouch stood up. "Can you believe that, I've crispified the little suckers! Yahoooooo!!!!!!!!"

Jan and Rain-bow moved quickly to collect the eggs, smiling and shaking their heads at Seezer and Ouch.

"Careful Jan," said Rain-bow. "I believe they could hatch at any time."

Jan took off her jacket and wrapped them up snug and secure. "Don't worry, I'll keep them safe. We'd better go now before those repulsive things come back."

As she turned, Jan saw a most stunning sight, leaving her speechless for a few moments. On a tree stump close to where Jan stood was a jar; it was full to the brim with rainbow coloured water in the middle of which was the fairy, sitting in a bubble. Jan suddenly remembered Seezer saying that fairies didn't like water and realised why the snotling had used it to imprison his captive.

"Oh my, it's a fairy! Look Rain-bow, it's a real fairy!"

Rain-bow smiled then looked back as Seezer and Ouch stepped up beside them. Ouch was more interested in getting his little brothers and sister and took the parcelled jacket from Jan. The big friendly dragon sniffed and cradled the eggs lovingly, snuggling them close beside his face.

Jan looked at him adoringly then, looking back at the jar, she opened it to release the imprisoned fairy. The bubble floated to the surface and popped with a strange, fluting sound and out she flew, sprinkling brilliant sparkles of light all around as she darted high in the sky, looped and came back down to rest on Jan's arm.

"Wow! You're beautiful." Jan was mesmerised at the sight before her. The fairy was a little thin girl with long flowing hair down to the backs of her legs. She was wearing a silky lilac dress and her wings had every colour of the rainbow on them.

Walking up and down Jan's arm she said, "Thank you, human. I will never forget this." And with a smile almost as big as her face, the grateful fairy shot into the sky and out of sight.

Gleaming trails of gold and silver showered over the four, who stood looking up after her. Suddenly, Seezer's head whipped round and his ears pricked up. "Quick, the others are on their way back and they're not happy! We have to get out of this forest fast!"

The friends took to their heels and fled, pushing on through the woods away from the returning snotlings, who would no doubt be exceptionally hungry as well as angry!

Praying that for once Ouch would be able to keep control of his feet until they were able to get out of the forest and take to the air, Jan pelted on as fast as she could. Lungs bursting, legs aching, she could hear the cries of the little creatures getting closer and closer behind them but she dare not look round. Their small size was an advantage in the confined space of the forest and their little wings helped them move at an incredible rate, pushing hard off the trunk of one tree and gliding several metres to the next.

Branches seemed to reach out to grab the friends and roots threatened to trip them up but somehow they kept going and kept ahead of the angry mob. At last Jan could see the trees ahead begin to thin and the sky was lighter as they reached the edge of the forest. Screaming as she felt a tiny hand grabbing her hair, Jan made one last enormous effort and threw herself forward beyond the tree line.

Relief came only when all four, with the eggs, were fully free of the forest. Running well clear of the trees, beyond the reach of any snotling hands or ropes, they all looked back and saw red evil little eyes dotted through the dark trees. Snotlings would never come out into the open without a plan; they were very vulnerable there as their small size and tiny wings were no longer an advantage, so the friends were finally safe.

But Ouch looked back once more; he did not like the look of the snotling leader, as it watched him with pure menace and hatred in his eyes. It was a look that the dragon would never forget and he shivered, sending ripples down his scaly back.

"Hey, we've come out on the other side of the forest!" said Rain-bow, looking around. "We're nearer Unicorn Island than your home now. I can still make that surprise visit to my parents. It'll be an even bigger surprise now, with all my friends here too!"

They walked onwards for a while until they finally felt safe enough to rest; they found a spot to sit down and catch their breath.

"My mum and dad are going to be so proud of me." Ouch rocked back and forth with his sibling eggs, then smacked his forehead with his hand. "Hey! My dad! He must still be in the forest looking for the eggs; we never saw him! I must go back and find him!"

Seezer went over to Ouch and, gravely, he said, "We can't go back in there. Those snotlings will tear us apart if we do and then your mum will have lost you and your brothers and sister too. The best thing now is to go on to Unicorn Island and ask for help. Your dad will be OK until we can get help; he can look after himself."

Rain-bow looked at them and said "To get to Unicorn Island we can either fly over the water or swim."

"I'm not a very strong swimmer," Jan said, doubtfully.

"Flying would be much quicker anyway," said Rain-bow, "but it means that Seezer will have to learn to fly with Ouch."

"I'm not very good at holding onto flying dragons!" cried Seezer as he looked over to Ouch.

The dragon looked disappointed. "Well, let's give it a go and we'll find out. We must get to Unicorn Island and get help as quickly as possible!"

Seezer rolled his eyes. "All right dragon, lie down."

Ouch stretched out and with one pounce, the wolf landed on his back. He circled and got into a steady position. "Now don't take off too fast," he warned.

Ouch slowly stood up and looked round at the wolf. "Don't worry friend, I won't drop you – on your head like your mother did!" And swiftly, without another word, the dragon took off into the air. Seezer gripped his paws into the scales of the dragon and held on for dear life. But the wolf needn't have worried. Ouch was clumsy on the ground, but very good in the air; he balanced his friend's weight on his back with ease. After a few loops and thrills, the dragon landed safely on the ground.

Seezer was shaken at first, and then narrowing his eyes, he jumped off and turned round to face Ouch. "Not so bad for a lounge lizard. Not so bad."

CHAPTER FOURTEEN

Up, Up and Away!

A few more trials and the group was under way, flying to Unicorn Island. Jan thought she had done everything possible that would count as unbelievable, but riding on a flying unicorn's back had to be the best!

All three eyes in Seezer's head were closed tight, as he didn't find the view as exciting as the others. The wolf was not used to being up high and could not wait for the landing. Rain-bow gave the sign and they began their decent to the marvellous island below. Unicorn Island was covered with tropical trees and cliffs with waterfalls and all of this was surrounded by a great marble wall. Outside of the wall, the island was fringed with wonderful sandy beaches. Gently, Ouch and Rain-bow landed on the soft sand and let their passengers get off.

"Amazing! Is that your home, Rain-bow?" Jan asked the white unicorn as she gazed at an enormous, beautifully carved wooden door set within the stone wall. "I suppose, if your dad's the King then you must be a princess."

"I guess I am, but I'm really just the same as all the others here. I never want, or ask, to be treated differently and nobody ever does. Unicorns are peaceful and loving and we really only want the best for life," she explained to Jan.

Jan listened with great interest. "I wish people could be like that."

Going from sand to marble, Rain-bow's hooves began to clip clop as they came up to the door. Jan looked up to see a unicorn watch them from high above the wall and, as if by magic, the heavy doors slowly opened.

Within the palace walls a spectacular site unfolded; a whole city of unicorns of all colours were going about their business. Jan gazed at pink unicorns with long golden mains and lilac and silver unicorns with bronze tails. Some baby unicorns played at a waterfall while others grazed under a magical rainbow, and she almost forgot why she was there.

Suddenly a trumpet sounded and all the unicorns cleared a path between the four visitors and the shiny marble ramp ahead of them.

"Can you all stay here please while I go and speak with my parents? I won't be long and you can have something to eat and drink." Rain-bow headed towards a winding path that led to an opening within the walls.

"Rain-bow, I know we have to find Ouch's dad first, but ... you won't forget the mirror, will you?" Jan cried after her.

The unicorn turned and smiled. "I won't forget, Jan."

Left behind, Rain-bow's friends fretted and worried, wishing there was something more that they could do. However, it was all down to Rain-bow now; only she could talk to her father and persuade him to mount a rescue mission for Ouch's father.

Suddenly there was a commotion in the palace above them and as they looked up at the source of the noise several magnificent, fierce-looking unicorns appeared and took off from a balcony in tight formation, flying off in the direction of the Forest.

"Oh, look!" breathed Jan. "Do you think they are going to rescue your dad, Ouch?"

"I hope so," said the dragon anxiously. He cradled the eggs in his arms, guarding them jealously.

Shortly after this, a very kind blue unicorn approached and asked Jan to go with her to Rain-bow and her family. All three friends started forwards but the blue unicorn stopped Ouch and Seezer.

"I'm sorry," she said. "At the moment, only Jan is invited. Please, stay here and enjoy our hospitality."

"But my dad!" cried Ouch. "What's happening? I need to find him!"

The blue unicorn assured him that all would be well; the unicorns who had just taken off were, as Jan had thought, a rescue party. The King had used the magic mirror to locate Ouch's dad. The snotlings were no match for a fully grown unicorn and, although usually peaceful as Rain-bow had said, a unicorn would never stand by and see an innocent creature suffer at the hands of evil. Therefore, the King had sent several of his best men to the forest, so it was certain that Ouch's dad would soon be home with his mum.

Ouch heaved an enormous sigh of relief, realising that his ordeal was finally over.

"Your mum and dad will both be so proud of you," said Jan.

"Yeah, and we are too," said Seezer, unexpectedly.

A surprised look came over Ouch and he moved to hug the wolf. Seezer jumped back.

"Whoa, back off dragon, don't you come near me..."

But it was too late. Ouch had carefully put down the eggs and scooped the wolf up, hugging him by his neck.

"Who's my buddy? Who's my best buddy?" he shouted happily.

Seezer gagged and squirmed. "Lemme go you big reptile, YUK!"

Laughing, Jan followed the blue unicorn and was taken into a pretty lemon-coloured room where Rain-bow stood nuzzling her mum.

At the other side of the room stood a very large white unicorn whose long golden unicorn horn was sparkling with embedded jewels. Jan could see rubies, emeralds and other precious stones and she knew this must be the King, Rain-bow's father.

As she arrived in front of him she said, "I don't know if I should curtsey, or what I should call you, your majesty," Jan said nervously. They all looked at each other and smiled.

"You can call me King Eon. As you know, I am Rain-bow's dad and please, try to relax Jan. No need to be so nervous. We have heard many good things about you and we will be forever grateful." The King walked closer to Jan. "I believe there is something we can do for you but first, will you talk with me alone for a few moments?"

Jan looked over to Rain-bow, who gave a reassuring nod.

"Yes, of course I will." Jan followed King Eon out to the balcony from which the rescue party had taken off earlier. They stood still and silent for a few moments as Jan took in the view of the beautiful island.

The King turned to look at Jan. "Dearest little human, before I leave you alone with the mirror can I ask you something?"

"Yes," Jan said without hesitating.

"Have you ever faced danger and been saved but you can't explain how?"

Jan looked confused. "I don't know what you mean sir."

"Think about the last time you said to yourself, *'that was close'* or *'that was lucky'*." The unicorn tilted his head to the side and looked deep into Jan's eyes.

After thinking for a moment, Jan cried, "I've got it! I remember one day, I was coming home from school and instead of taking the long way home, I climbed up on to a wall that ran between two houses. The ground on one side came half way up the wall, but on the other side it was a very long drop. I was half way across when a big angry black dog came running at me on the low side of the wall. He was going to bite me, I just know he was." Jan shivered as she remembered the fear of that moment.

"Well, what happened?" the King asked her.

"I looked down to the other side of the wall and thought about jumping, but it was too high and I would have broken my legs or my neck for sure. It seemed like there were only two options; get torn to pieces or jump and risk dying. I didn't realise there was a third option.

Then, out of nowhere, a big white dog came running from the other direction and chased the black dog. I remember thinking how lucky I was that the white dog was there. The two dogs began to fight and believe me, I ran to the end of that wall very quickly and climbed down."

The royal stallion smiled down at her little face.

"Is that the kind of thing you mean?" Jan asked him.

"Yes, that's exactly it. Now, on the table over there is the mirror. Look deep into it and you will see what you need to. I will leave you to it." And with that, the large unicorn King walked away.

Pure excitement ran through every part of Jan. She was scared but happy at the same time. She was going to see her grandmother again. Hesitantly at first, she went over to the table and found a red cloth covering what must be the mirror. She pulled it off nervously and looked into the mirror. Seeing only her own reflection, she concentrated harder, looking deeper and deeper into the glass.

"Oh, Granma!" Jan jumped back, tears rolling down her face. She moved closer again. In the mirror, she could see her grandmother, surrounded by a white mist that swirled all around her. Granma was telling her how proud she was and that no matter what, she would always be there for her.

Jan leaned further towards the mirror and listened more carefully. Granma was saying that, even though she was no longer physically there, she would always be watching over her and when she least expected it, would guide her and guard her through her life. "Jan, listen to me very carefully," the wise old lady told her granddaughter. "One thing I regret never telling you was this, don't ever stop daydreaming no matter what! I know this past while you have shown great restraint in keeping your imagination in check. And you have improved in your school work and general behaviour, but Jan it's your ability to dream of the impossible that makes you so special. Many children have been told that they are wasting their lives away because their heads are in the clouds, but this simply isn't true. Parents and teachers all over the world are now realising that it is these children who are our future. These dreamers become the inventors, authors and people who break through the barriers of the impossible. They just need to learn when it's OK to daydream and when you need to concentrate on other things. Jan, never give up on your dreams........"

The image was fading and the words were getting fainter. Jan could still see her grandmother faintly and hear her whispering in her ear, "Live a great life Jan, full of adventures and amazing journeys. Be happy....... I will always be with you................"

The mirror finally went dark and Jan realised she had been holding her breath. She took in a large breath of air and, sobbing, she clutched at the mirror with both hands.

"Jan," a voice behind her said. Startled, she turned round and ran to hug her unicorn friend.

"Oh Rain-bow, I saw Granma, I saw her!"

Jan wiped her eyes as the Unicorn King said, "Jan, do you understand what your grandmother was saying to you?"

She looked up to meet his gaze. "She wants me to be happy and will always be watching over me."

63

"More than that. When you were saved from that black dog, when you were young, someone from the other side must have been watching over you. This is what your grandmother is saying to you; live your life to the full Jan Otters, cherish your memories of your grandmother and be happy. But someone as special as you will always be watched over and influenced to do the right thing in difficult situations. And your imagination will allow you to see solutions to problems that other people may never be able to see."

"Thank you. I think I understand now. Granma would hate me to waste my life, crying and worrying all the time."

Rain-bow nestled her long velvety face next to Jan's neck. "It's all right to cry sometimes, Jan, but now that you feel a bit better, you can be strong for your family."

"Yes! My mum and dad, I must get back to them. I need to support them now."

After thanking the unicorn family for their help, Jan and her three friends set off back to Ouch's family. They flew a long time over land and water before finally landing at the dragon caves.

Ouch ran to hug his mum and dad, weeping tears of joy this time. Ouch's parents were over the moon at the safe return of all their babies – including Ouch! – and planned a big party to celebrate.

But Jan was not in the mood to party. As much as she was happy for everyone, she had realised that she needed to get home and face up to the situation with her family. She knew a lot of words had to be spoken and healing had to take place. This was not going to be an easy time for her family to go through, but she felt stronger and more able to deal with it, and to help her family to also come to terms with things.

So once more, she set out with her friends for the hill top where the Fire-Tree stood. Jan marvelled again at the magnificent sight of the tree, the branches bearing orange and gold flames instead of leaves, yet never burning.

When Ouch returned from the tree with the burning branch that would help him return Jan home, he gave Jan a small twig to put in her pocket.

"What's this for?" Jan hesitated to take it, as the twig still had smoke coming from it. "Is it hot?"

"No, it's only a small twig so it has cooled down quickly. Keep it in your pocket, Jan, and if you ever need me, rub it until it warms up, then make a wish for me to come get you or for you to come to me."

Jan hugged her friends and found it was harder to leave them this time than the last. She realised she loved them but she needed the love of her family more right now.

With a nod of readiness, she fell back into her strange journey of swirling colour and before she knew it, she was opening her eyes in the janitor's closet.

As before, when she opened the door, Jan realised that no time had passed on Earth and she was right back where she began. Although she was worried about how to get away unseen, leaving the school was easier than she thought and she ran all the way home. Exhausted, she pushed open the front door.

"Jan, oh my darling, where have you been?"

And with that, Jan was surrounded by her family, hugging and loving her, just the way it should be.

Sometime later, Jan went upstairs and stood in the doorway of her grandmother's bedroom, undecided about whether to enter. It had been her own bedroom until Granma had come to stay with them and Jan had been relegated to the couch, but her mum promised her she wouldn't have to move back until she was ready. Jan wasn't sure when that would be exactly but she did feel a lot better.

She put her hands in her pockets and leaned on the door frame. Touching something in her pocket, she pulled it out and stared at the twig that Ouch had given her.

'I wonder if I will ever use it?' she thought. But somehow she already knew the answer.

PART III

CHAPTER FIFTEEN

Valentine's Dragon

It was mid September; Jan was now twelve years old and she had recently started up at the big school. She was a first-year student at Summerhall Academy and, despite her initial anxiety, what a thrill the past month had turned out to be. She had made new friends, finally discovered her way around the huge school and, to cap it all, met the love of her life! His name was Maxwell Gettem and Jan had got a nasty shock when she discovered that he was the older brother of Sheila Gettem, one of the girls who used to bully Jan at primary school. He was so gorgeous though and Jan was sure he couldn't be anything like his sister. Surely no family could be unlucky enough to have two selfish, bullying idiots like that! No, Maxwell must be kind and gentle. What a shame he had to put up with Sheila as a sister!

The first time she had seen him, she was working at the school snack shop at break-time. Their hands touched, their eyes met and Jan was hooked! Her heart skipped a beat and she knew she would never be the same again.

"Dreamy or what?" she had asked Lucy, one of her best friends.

"All right if you like that sort of tall, footbally, sporty kind of older boy," her friend had replied with a grin. Actually, Maxwell was only a year older than Jan and to her he was heaven on a plate. She desperately wanted him to notice her.

Jan's opportunity came a few months later when she found out about the forthcoming Valentine's Day Dance in the school hall.

"Next Friday!" she shrieked. "I'll never save enough money by then to buy a dress." Jan now had a paper round, but the next 2 weeks' money would never be enough for a nice dress. In low spirits and naturally overreacting, it felt to the young girl as if her life was in ruins. It felt like this was her one chance to impress the boy of her dreams; if she couldn't make a good impression at the dance it would all be over. If he noticed or remembered Jan Otters at all, it would probably be as the shabbily clad, unfashionable girl wearing last year's clothes!

Jan's friends sympathised with her feelings of ultra-hideousness but weren't about to allow her to be sad for the rest of the day. Lucy Small and Roland Ball had been Jan's

66

friends since primary school and had seen her through some tough times, particularly when they were all being bullied and when Jan's grandmother had died.

Making sure that the other children in the playground could not hear them, Lucy, knowing that Jan's parents didn't have a lot of money and that Jan wouldn't be able to get a new dress for the dance, suggested loaning her an outfit.

"We can make a night of it. You both come round to my house tonight and we'll have a fashion show," Lucy said with a big smile.

Although Roland, being best friends with two girls and not wishing to cause offence, had put up with these kinds of girly nights before, he avoided them if he could. So, rolling his eyes, he opted out in favour of another attempt to cross-breed his pet turtle with a recently purchased tortoise. He dreamed that his claim to fame would be as the creator of the PET-TORTTUL, which was just one of many strange ideas the boy had.

Jan thanked Lucy for her kind and thoughtful offer but, embarrassed, reminded her that she wasn't allowed to borrow clothes. Her parents were rather proud and didn't like the thought of accepting hand-outs; they had always taught Jan to accept what she was and never try to be anything different. "It's what's inside that counts," they would tell her.

"Anyway," Jan said humbly, recalling her parents' wise words and trying hard to convince herself as much as her friend, "if Maxwell Gettem likes me half as much as I like him, then it won't matter about my outfit for the dance."

Unfortunately, the three friends didn't notice Sheila Gettem and Camilla Pitts listening in on their conversation. The two horrid girls were hiding round the corner and were absolutely delighted to have such juicy information fall accidentally right into their mischievous little hands. They may have turned over a new leaf at primary school and given up their bullying ways, but this was too good a chance to miss! Besides, they had a whole new set of people to try to impress now...

It felt like the Friday night of the dance had taken simply ages to arrive and all the school pupils were excited as they lined up outside the entrance to the school.

Large cut-outs of red and pink love hearts lined the path of the queue, which contained chatty girls who smelled of perfume and boys trying to act very cool. Everyone had made an effort, with party clothes and fancy hairstyles; it was a very colourful scene and the students were buzzing with anticipation.

Jan was standing in line beside Roland and they were getting anxious that Lucy hadn't appeared yet. She was wearing her hand-me-down dress from last year and that wouldn't have bothered Jan so much, but to her great disappointment a humongous spot had appeared on the end of her nose!

Knowing how important the evening was to Jan, her mum had dabbed the spot with concealer make-up, trying her best to hide it, but it was a lost cause. It was enormous; Jan felt that the revolting zit was like having another head growing out of her face and nothing could make it better. Of all the times in her life to be presented with her first spot, why on earth did it have to be now!

It didn't matter anymore anyway because earlier that day, Jan had found out that she had been nominated for snack shop duty at the dance, so any chance of having enough time to build up the courage to approach Maxwell Gettem was well and truly over. Most of her time would be taken up by serving sugar-based snacks to the other children, who would really be enjoying themselves. It seemed like everything was going against her and it was so unfair!

Just then, Jan felt someone prodding her on the back and turned round to see who it was, expecting it to be Lucy. It wasn't her though; Jan's eyes popped when she saw who it was.

"Maxwell Gettem, oh my goodness, eh, eh, I mean, what do you want?"

Jan was kicking herself for reacting like such a silly dithering little girl and inside she promised herself that she would learn to string a sentence together as soon as the shock of this gorgeous boy looking into her face was over.

"Hi Jan." Maxwell flicked a confident, wicked little grin from the side of his face and handed her a note. "For you babe." He continued to smile at her over his shoulder as he strutted to the front of the queue.

Jan was convinced that the stupid gormless look on her face should be slapped off with a hand the size of a bus but she quickly snapped back to level-headedness over the realisation of the note.

Lucy appeared at that moment; bounding towards them with eyes wide open she said, "What did he give you Jan?"

Looking at both her friends in turn, Jan shrugged her shoulders and tapped her nose as if to say it was none of their business. When no answer was forthcoming, both Lucy and Roland quickly got fed up waiting and turned their back on her.

When Jan realised that no one was looking, she unfolded the note with shaking hands. Her heart flipped when she saw a love heart on the corner of the paper and she quickly began reading.

Dear Jan,
I fancy you and need to see you tonight so we can have our first snog! Meet me in the janitor's closet behind the snack shop at 9.00pm.
P.S. come alone and don't tell anyone.
MOST IMPORTANT – DON'T turn on the lights. Let our lips find each other!
Luv and hugs - your hunny bunny xxxxxxx

68

With her heart still racing, she finished reading, quickly folded the note up and put it in her pocket. She could hardly believe it but at last something seemed to be going right for her! The very thing she had longed for since that first meeting at the snack shop and now it turned out he had been feeling the same thing! This was a wonderful secret that she must keep all to herself, at least for now. She would tell her two friends later.

Roland looked over his shoulder to Jan and shook his head in disappointment. He was clearly upset that she wouldn't tell him what the note said and told her that in his opinion, Maxwell probably wrote something sick and vile and that Jan shouldn't trust him.

Jan ignored her friends' disapproval because she felt like she was floating on air and was sure she was about to have the best night of her life! Even the prospect of snack shop duty couldn't dampen her spirits now; she would definitely be making the most of the rest of her time!

The main doors opened and light spilled from the open doors onto the students in the queue, together with the sound of distant music. A frenzy of noisy and excitable teenagers pushed through the doors and rushed along the corridors to the dance area. As they entered the hall, Roland threw his coat onto a chair in the corner and sat down, heaving a heavy sigh. Accepting the fact that he would be on his own all night, he muttered under his breath to himself, "Why would anyone dance with me anyway? I'm fat and ugly!"

Actually, Roland Ball was a very handsome boy; he just didn't have any confidence in himself because he was slightly chunky around the waist. He was also a bit of a know-it-all and swamped himself in books and geeky hobbies. Although Lucy and Jan were his friends, he could never tell them that secretly, he would love to have a girlfriend. He just pretended that all that romance stuff was disgusting.

Out of nowhere, a small boy appeared in front of Roland. The freckled lad just stood there staring up at Roland with one finger up his nose and one hand in his pocket. Roland shrugged his shoulders, shook his head and said, *"And!"* The boy handed him a note from his pocket. Roland took the note from the boy, then puzzled, looked back at the boy who now had his finger up the other side of his nose. Roland recognised the boy as Connor Edwards from primary school, but he'd never been friends with him. The boy told him, still with finger up his nose, that a girl had pointed Roland out from across the hall and paid him with a packet of fizz bombs to deliver a folded note. Roland was confused as to why a girl would send *him* a secret message. The boy turned to go away, suddenly chewing on something, and Roland, totally grossed out by the thought of what the boy must be eating, quickly unfolded the piece of paper to read it.

After reading the note, Roland scrunched it up and tossed it over his shoulder, pulling a face and feeling more miserable than ever. "Stupid kids", he said to himself, convinced that someone was playing a childish joke on him.

CHAPTER SIXTEEN

A kiss to forget

Jan was allowed one hour to take part in the Valentine's dance before her duty at the snack shop began and she wanted to make the most of it. She couldn't understand why Maxwell Gettem would fancy her, especially when the spot on her nose felt like it could be seen from outer space, but happiness was happiness and she was going to grab it with both hands.

Disco lights were flashing and music played as Jan and Lucy danced by the far wall, lined with chairs. Roland seemed to be having less of a good time and no matter how many times they both tried to pull him up to dance, he was having none of it. He just sat in the corner with his arms folded, glowering at the dance floor. He seemed preoccupied with something, but wouldn't tell Jan or Lucy what it was.

Lucy had forgiven her best friend for not sharing her secret with her, because Jan promised to tell her all about it after the dance. "He's sitting there like a grumpy old man," Lucy bawled into Jan's ear, trying to be heard over the loud music.

"Let's go out to the corridor; I can't hear you," Jan screamed back.

Leaving the pulsating beat behind them with ears ringing, the girls walked out of the hall, giggling and smiling, when they spotted Mr Goodfellow, the Head Teacher. He was checking over the snack shop stand and when he saw them, he beckoned to them to come over.

"Having a good time girls?" he enquired. Mr Goodfellow was the best head teacher ever and he was very fair; everyone said so. If you were ever in any trouble, he would wait until he had heard both sides of the story before doing anything and he always said that he was proud of his school pupils. Jan had loved his speech in the hall on the first day she arrived at the academy – she found him very inspiring and a definite improvement on Mrs Whip, Jan's primary head teacher.

"We are having so much fun." Jan turned to Lucy and linked arms with her as she nodded in agreement.

Mr Goodfellow smiled at them. "Good. Now I believe you are going to take care of everyone tonight. Mr Aberdeen, our janitor, says that you're the very one to entrust with our confectionery goods. Here is the cash box and I will go and make the necessary announcements." And off he went into the hall to herd up the awaiting stampede of break-time chocolate munchers.

Lucy tried to sneak away. "Oh no you don't. You can't leave me Lucy. Stay and help, please?" Jan said, grabbing her friends' hand and tilting a begging head to one side.

"All right, but I want a free snack out of this," Lucy insisted. However, she had no intention of staying for long and missing out on all the fun.

Sometime later, the rush was over and the masses had been fed. They'd queued, they'd bought and they'd eaten as if they urgently needed the sugar for dance energy. Jan kept looking at her watch impatiently.

"Why do you keep looking at your watch? Do you have to go home early or something?" Lucy asked.

"No, it's just ... oh nothing. Thanks for helping me, I really appreciate it. You can go back into the hall and enjoy the rest of the dance. I'll put all the boxes back into the janitor's closet by myself."

Lucy hesitated, suspicious of her friend's sudden change of heart about wanting help, but she was eager to dance the last hour away so she accepted the offer and hurried back to the hall.

Jan glanced at her watch once more. It was 8.50pm and her heart began to race. She tidied all the chocolate cartons and crisp boxes swiftly away in the closet. The Head had already collected the cash box, so she was set. She closed the door and rushed to the girls' cloak room to check her face in the mirror.

'Oh fudge!' she thought as she gazed into the mirror, 'why did this ugly blemish have to exist?' Looking closer at her reflection, Jan consoled herself by remembering the scraggly little urchin she used to be back in primary school. Now, however, it was as plain as the spot on the end of her nose that her looks had matured and improved a little. Her long bronze curls, which had always been so wild and unkempt in primary school, were sleeker now and cascaded around her heart-shaped face, framing an unknowing green-eyed beauty.

Staring into her very soul made Jan drift off into one of her daydreams and in her mind she imagined a space rocket taking off. Once it had broken through the atmosphere the spaceship slowed down and the astronauts floated about in zero gravity.

Suddenly, panic stations as one of the astronauts grabbed the radio control and said; "Houston, we have a problem, we cannot see the Great Wall of China, I repeat, something is blocking the view of the Great Wall of China. Hold on – wait a moment, it seems to be due to a young girl's acne problem. Yes, that's what it is all right. Don't worry Houston, if we can't land at the Kennedy Space Centre, we can always land on this super-sized zit!"

Jan chuckled to herself at the thought but quickly returned to reality at the realisation of her impending 'life changing moment'. Shrugging her shoulders and realising there was nothing she could do about the spot, she took a deep breath. A smear of lip gloss, dab of perfume behind the ears, a swift brush of her hair and back Jan sprinted to the janitor's closet.

Before going in to the small room, she looked around to make sure nobody was in sight and checked her watch. One minute to go.

The light switch was on the outside wall; out of habit she started reaching towards it but managed to stop herself, remembering the note. What if Maxwell was already in the closet? The note said that their lips would find each other, so she went in quickly, closing the door behind her and shutting out all light.

She was breathing fast and could almost hear her heart pounding in her ears. Suddenly there was a noise as something stirred. There *was* someone else already in the closet!

Jan remembered the time when Ouch the dragon had been hiding behind her in the janitor's closet at her primary school. The thought of the sweet dragon made her smile; she really missed him.

A sudden sharp noise like something being nudged and then a sound like someone coming towards her made the image of her dear friend quickly disappear. Listening carefully, Jan could make out slow, shuffling footsteps as someone felt their way towards her in the utter darkness, and then a hand reached out and grabbed her elbow!

Despite the fact that this was exactly what she had been hoping for, Jan jumped. However, the hand did not let go; instead the person began to move closer to her and Jan held her breath as someone, breathing deeply, came to within a few inches of her face.

Lips were about to meet as promised, and suddenly Jan felt extremely nervous that her first kiss with Maxwell Gettem was about to become a reality.

All at once, the overhead strip lights flickered on, blinding them after the total blackness and both struggled to adjust to the sudden brightness as they stepped back and tried to make out each other's face. At the same time, the closet door flew open.

Jan's world came slowly crashing down around her and she stood rooted to the spot, staring in terror as outside the door stood Maxwell Gettem and what looked like every other child in school. Her eyes narrowed in disbelief as explosions of laughter blasted straight at her.

So if Maxwell was out there then who was she about to kiss? Jan's head snapped round to look at the person standing beside her.

Totally shock-stricken she cried, "Roland, what are you doing in here? How...? What...?"

The waves of laughter from all around were crushing and the humiliating realisation that the whole school had just played a cruel prank on her made her whole body cringe in shame. First, the colour drained from her face turning her very pale, and then it was quickly replaced by a beetroot red colour of pure embarrassment.

Seeing her torture, Roland closed the door quickly to protect Jan and himself from further ridicule. Tears streamed down Jan's face and she leaned against the wall in total misery and despair.

"I had nothing to do with it Jan, I promise you. They played a trick on me too. Connor Edwards gave me a note that said Erin McFyfe fancied me and I had to kiss her in the closet at 9 o'clock. I knew it was too good to be true. Why the heck do I have to be so gullible all the time?"

Jan looked up at him through her tears and, sighing, nodded her head. "Now I get it. I bet your note said that you shouldn't turn on the lights and that lips would find each other."

Frowning, Roland nodded, looking genuinely heart-broken. He was used to being laughed at because of his size, but that didn't mean it didn't hurt! On top of that, he hated what they were doing to his friend. He wasn't a violent boy but he felt like he could tear them all apart for doing this to her.

Outside, Sheila and Maxwell Gettem switched off the closet light "To give the lovebirds some privacy!" they shouted, and led the others in a chorus of chanting;

Jan and Roland,

Valentine's is here,

Pity you're so ugly,

Your kids will die of fear!

Finding themselves in the dark again, Jan sighed with disappointment. Maxwell and Sheila Gettem were obviously just as bad as each other, after all! How could she have thought he could possibly be any better than his sister? "Why are they so cruel Roland? Didn't they put us through enough of this at primary school?"

"Never mind them, Jan. It's big school now and the level of cruelty has gone up a notch. Let's hold our heads up, walk out of here and go home." Roland, trying to seem braver than he felt and understanding that they had to face the others some time, was ready to open the door. But Jan stopped him.

"No, I can't. I can never face them again. I just want to....."

"You want to what?" he asked.

Jan had an idea but it could not involve her friend. Desperation made her think of Ouch her dragon friend, and she needed to get to Zoogly quickly. The young girl questioned herself, as she knew she couldn't keep running away from her problems like this, but she needed time to think and gather her strength before she faced the horrid gathering outside.

Time away in her magic world was just what she needed to help get over the awkwardness of the past few moments. She remembered coming back from her past journeys from the other world before and had been amazed to discover that no time had actually passed on her side, so what did she have to lose? It seemed like the perfect solution; some time out to compose herself and let the hurt pass, while for everyone else it would seem like she had taken it all in her stride.

"Jan, are you all right?" There was a thin trickle of light creeping in from under the door; their eyes were becoming accustomed to the dark and Roland could just make out Jan's outline. He was concerned as his friend seemed rather distant and was acting peculiarly.

"Yes, I'm fine, but I need you to do something for me. Promise me that you will?"

"You know I will do anything for you Jan, but you're scaring me. What are you going to do?"

"I need you to go to the far corner, face the wall and whatever happens, don't look round for a few minutes, no matter what, promise?"

"But I don't get it, what are ………"

Jan put her fingers up to cover his mouth. "Please Roland; more than anything in the world, I need you to do this."

Shrugging his shoulders, he reluctantly felt his way over to the far side of the closet, turned to the wall and closed his eyes. "Go on then, whatever it is hurry up."

Jan felt in her dress pocket for the little twig she always carried around with her. Since Ouch the dragon had given it to her over a year ago, she had kept it with her always, like a good luck charm. She didn't feel very lucky after what had just happened though, so she hoped against hope that its powers had not faded!

Thinking back to the instructions she was given at the end of her last quest, she began to rub the little twig until it felt warm in her hand. This small part of the Fire-Tree had been broken off and given to her as a way to come back if she ever needed to. In her mind, she was wishing she was in the land of Zoogly, over and over again.

Within moments, the familiar feeling of falling through the air rushed back to Jan; she knew she was on her way and it felt good. Then, suddenly, a hand came out to grab her shoulder and she could hear Roland shouting after her as though from a great distance.

Whirls of colour spiralled up from the ground and wrapped around her as she sped dizzily into another world. Unlike the previous entry into this amazing magic kingdom, Jan was not gently held and cradled by her dragon friend's arms; this landing hurt her bottom with a smack!

"Yikes!" an unexpected voice said behind her.

'Oh dear,' she thought, assuming she must have hurt someone when she landed. Hoping to see Ouch the dragon, she turned round quickly and stopped, startled by what she saw.

"Roland! Oh my goodness, what are you doing here?"

CHAPTER
SEVENTEEN

A jealous friend

Roland looked around him in bewilderment. There were fields, trees, hills – nothing out of the ordinary, all other things being equal, except weren't they supposed to be in a closet at school? Confused about his location, he looked up at the sky and his jaw dropped as he saw two moons in a very strange sky. "Jan, where on earth are we?" He screwed up his face and looked at Jan for an answer.

Nervously, Jan wondered for a moment how to handle the situation but decided that there was nothing she could do but tell the truth. However, whether Roland would believe it or not was a different matter. "Actually, we're not on earth, at least we were until I made a wish in the janitor's closet and now we are in Zoogly."

"I don't understand. One minute you were falling back in the closet and I went to catch you, the next minute we're here! Is this a dream? What was that Zoogly thing you said?" He stared at her as she raised one eyebrow and shook her head.

"I realise that this must be a shock to you but before you meet my friends, I think I should tell you something or you may go into shock permanently."

Jan told Roland that this was her third time in Zoogly and explained how she first arrived after being transported from the janitor's closet back in primary school when she was ten years old.

She went on to explain how Sheila Gettem and Camilla Pitts had locked her in the closet after seeing her go in to return a bucket and mop. At the same time as this was going on, a scared dragon in Zoogly had wished at the Fire-Tree for someone to come and help stop a three-headed fuzzbutt monster from bullying him and his friends at school.

Jan remembered falling over the mop in the dark just before she had been whisked into the other dimension; she had thought she had hit her head. The only way she got through her first adventure in Zoogly was because she thought she was in a coma and dreaming! Jan's grandmother had been in a coma for a while and had dreamed of another world and amazing creatures like these, so Jan had assumed that the same thing had happened to her.

Jan reminded Roland that he, Jan and Lucy were being bullied by a group of horrible girls in primary school and she felt that this had something to do with why her dream felt so familiar. She had later realised that this may have been the very reason why the Fire-Tree had chosen her to come and help! She had the knowledge and the power inside her all along to deal with the bullies, but had needed something to show her that she did.

At the time, she had just put it down to her subconscious making it up. After the adventure, she had talked about it to her grandmother a lot, until Granma had died. That's when she had realised that she hadn't been dreaming after all, as Ouch had appeared in the closet, needing Jan's help again, and Jan was fully conscious!

A kind of liberation washed over Jan as she realised that now she had someone to share her amazing secret world with. It had been wonderful to talk to Granma about it, but that had been when Jan believed it was a dream. She had never realised it was real until Granma was gone, so she had never been able to share it fully with her. Relieved and beginning to enjoy the thrill, she continued to put her friend in the picture about her adventures, but he just looked at her as if she were going mad.

"And to top it all, this magnificent kingdom full of castles, lakes and mountains is all suspended in time and space and rides on the back of a beautiful butterfly." Jan was finally out of breath.

Roland collapsed back down to a sitting position and stared up at Jan as if weakness had taken over as a result of all the very strange things Jan was telling him. Jan was actually finding this all very amusing and inside, she was bubbling up with the excitement of having another human to share her fantastic cloak-and-dagger double life with. It had been over a year since she had lost Granma, and that was a long time to keep quiet. The satisfaction that this more than made up for not telling him what the silly little note from Maxwell had said earlier on made her feel somewhat proud.

Jan decided that this was enough information for now and finished off by saying, "Don't fight it because you'll go crazy if you do. Best accept it like I did and then we can have some fun."

"Fun? You think this is fun? You're telling me that we've just been transported to another world, through the janitor's closet if you don't mind, and you want me to just accept that?" Roland stood up and began to walk away.

"Roland, wait for me! You can't just walk into Zoogly on your own. They don't know you." Her voice became harsher with annoyance as she tried to catch up. "I mean it Roland, hold on or you're going to be in for a big surprise!"

Roland stopped in his tracks and turned round to face her. "Oh I'm so scared. Ooooooooowww a big dragon is going to surprise me and gobble me all up. Really

Jan, I didn't get top marks all through school for nothing you know, so stop making all this up. It's really starting to tick me off!"

But Jan wasn't listening; she had a large grin on her face and was looking beyond Roland at the big dragon coming in to land right behind her unsuspecting friend's head.

"Ouch!" Jan cried as her eyes began to fill with tears of joy. Seeing her friend again had made her realise just how much she had missed him.

Roland stepped back and wondered why Jan had cried out in pain. Did not believing her story hurt her feelings that much? And why was she looking right through him and ... how come he had just bumped into something warm and solid behind him?

Eyes still on Jan, he felt behind him with his hands. A strange smoky smell reached his nostrils and he started to twitch his nose. At the same time, his hair blew back and forth; some kind of deep breathing was going on above his head. Gulping and slightly nervous, he forced himself to turn around to see what was behind him.

First, Roland saw a scaly red belly then, swallowing again and tilting his head back, he looked up to see an impressive dragon's head with a large grin upon its face. When their eyes met, however, the dragon's smile changed to a thin, thoughtful line and his bright blue eyes narrowed to study the boy.

Fear drenched Roland from head to foot and the trembling boy immediately pulled Jan in front of him for protection.

Ouch the dragon glanced swiftly at Jan then winked one eye in a playful manner. The dragon raised a claw up to his face, bared large teeth and blew a little flame onto his plump dragon finger, which stayed there, dancing in the breeze. He then put the flaming finger into his mouth and extinguished the flame, while lowering his head to Roland's eye level. Ouch opened his lips just enough to make a small circle shape and puffed out rings of black smoke – right into Roland's face. Narrowing his eyes again, and with a deeper voice than Jan had remembered the dragon having, he spoke in a low husky voice. "So you're not surprised are you? Well you should be." Ouch straightened up and towered above Roland, flexing his magnificent purple wings. "Who invited you into my world anyway?"

Roland was shaking worse than ever and all colour seemed to drain from his body. It was funny at first but Jan had had enough and felt for the position Roland was being put into. "Stop it Ouch, you'll scare him to death!"

The dragon gave the boy one more menacing look, then turned to Jan and began to smile. "Oh Jan it's so good to see you. I've been back to the closet for you several times but you just weren't there anymore."

Jan hugged her big reptilian buddy, noting that her arms couldn't reach quite as far round him as they could before. "I've moved up to the big school, but I'm here now." Like long lost friends, they reached out and held on to each other, soaking in the reunion for a few moments.

Finally, Ouch stepped back and looked her up and down, his nostrils still filled with the fantastic smell from behind Jan's ears that he had never known before. "Yes, you are much taller but just as pretty as I remember."

Jan's face went bright red as she put her hand over her nose and tried to hide the big spot on the end of it. She was flattered at the dragon's kind words and coyly turned to the side to look at Roland, whose face was now contorted with a mixture of anxiety and bafflement of the everyday chit chat that was going on before him. Jan suddenly realised that he was in need of some reassurance from her that the dragon wasn't going to hurt him, but she wanted to return the compliment to Ouch first.

"You have definitely got bigger too; stretch out your wings for me."

Ouch straightened up and with a soft swishing noise, flipped out his superb purple wings. When folded, they could barely be seen at his sides but when he unfurled them they now stretched out longer than his body. He looked at Jan from the corner of his eye and proudly raised his head up further. "What do you think," he asked her. "Impressive or what?"

Jan smiled and her heart seemed to skip a beat. The full impact of missing him suddenly dawned on her. Stretching up onto her tip toes, she extended her arms up to touch his face and looked lovingly into his big blue eyes. "You could give a three-headed fuzzbutt monster a run for its money."

The dragon pulled in a large satisfying breath; this was the best compliment anyone could ever give him as a fuzzbutt monster was very nasty and strong; especially the mutant three-headed one that they both knew! There was much history here between the two as they had shared a couple of great adventures that could never be forgotten. It was hard for them to break eye contact and it was obvious that the pair had missed each other dreadfully.

A coughing noise suddenly brought them back to the situation at hand and they both turned to look at Roland.

"Oh, I am so sorry. Ouch, this is Roland, my friend from school. Roland, this is Ouch, my best friend, the one I was trying to tell you about."

The realisation that Jan had merely called him a friend, compared to a big dragon that she called her best friend, hurt Roland and he took an instant dislike to the fire-breathing creature.

Ouch gave the human boy a quick sideways glance and the dragon also felt an uncomfortable moment between the two of them. Jan looked back and forth between her two friends. She had a feeling that it would take some time before there was any trust here but she was determined not to let it spoil things. She was back in the land of Zoogly where great things could happen and she was definitely looking forward to them.

Jan began to walk on and asked Ouch where he had been flying to when he had spotted her and Roland from the air. He told her that he had been returning from visiting Seezer the snow wolf before he set off on a trip to Unicorn Island to meet with Rain-bow. Rain-bow was a wonderful unicorn who had befriended Jan and had also been one of Jan's class-mates on her first adventure to Zoogly. The beautiful winged pony was rescued by Jan, Ouch and Seezer from evil forest snotlings on Jan's second adventure and in return, she had helped Jan deal with the heartache of losing Granma. Through the power of an enchanted mirror, the kind unicorn enabled Jan to see her one more time and finally feel at peace, coming to terms with her loss.

Jan asked how Seezer and Rain-bow both were as she remembered them with great fondness; on her last adventure to Zoogly, they had all become very close. They were both on Unicorn Island and as Ouch had other commitments at this time, Jan was sad to learn that they wouldn't be able to go and see them on this adventure.

Roland was feeling a bit left out as he listened to the unlikely pair talking about their past adventures together. "So, what amazing quest have you got planned for Jan this time Dragon?" he interrupted.

Ouch looked down at the dark-haired boy. "You can call me Ouch and what I have planned for Jan is none of your business!"

Jan's head shot up. "Ouch, it wasn't his fault, it's mine. Roland is here by accident and as long as he is here, he will have to come everywhere with us. I can't just leave him. You understand don't you?"

The dragon paused, then rolled his eyes and nodded reluctantly. "All right, I suppose. Now, if you are looking for an adventure there is a big party at Star Lake and you are – I mean you are both, invited to come to the Heart-Pairing evening."

Jan looked excited. "What's the Heart-Pairing evening all about?"

Ouch looked over to Roland as he said, "It's where the best boys pair with the best girls and have their first kiss!"

"Oh, I see." Jan didn't like the sound of this and explained to Ouch what had just happened back in the janitor's closet before they arrived in Zoogly. However, she didn't want to dwell on that or spoil the happy reunion, so she quickly changed the subject. She could see that her protective dragon friend was furious with how she had been treated back at school.

"And who are you going to be kissing, you handsome dragon?" Jan asked, expecting him to brush the question aside and say that he wasn't kissing anyone. But she was disappointed. As if a red dragon could not become any more red, his cheeks began to deepen to the colour of dark smouldering lava.

Ouch stopped and twisted his body while looking down at his big clumsy feet. He looked away into the distance and said, "Her name is Oops and she is the most beautiful blue dragon I have ever seen. Do you remember her, Jan? She sat beside us in class on your first visit here."

Jan's heart sank as she heard the news. It upset her strangely but she didn't understand why it made her feel that way. Of course Ouch should have an admirer; he was kind and gentle and a very handsome dragon. But why did the news make her wish she hadn't come to Zoogly this time?

CHAPTER EIGHTEEN

The City of Zoogly

Jan, Ouch and Roland had walked through the countryside and now the magnificent city of Zoogly lay before them. The main street stretched on for a mile and tall castle-like buildings lined both sides. Beyond the roof tops stood splendid snow-tipped mountains and at their base the entrances to a deep labyrinth of twisting inner-city caves could be seen. Looking high past the orange and red sky that permanently surrounded the kingdom, stars twinkled in the black canvas of space above a very unusual planet.

Zoogly was built and carried on the back of a beautiful giant butterfly that was suspended in space and time. The gentle flutter of its wings, so slow as to be almost motionless, sent a warm breeze throughout the land, where night never truly fell.

As the two humans and the dragon walked into the city, they became aware of the curious glances being cast their way from strange-looking creatures. Jan had seen most of them before on her previous visits but Roland was in total awe and his eyes could not take it in quickly enough.

"Wow, this is amazing Jan!" The bewildered boy nearly fell over several times while gawking at unicorns, wolves and the most bizarre of all, the Zooglies, the main inhabitants of the city. Zooglies were round in shape, half the size of a human and sported shocking green Mohican spiky hair that went well with their even more shocking, large, wonky eyes. They had little thin arms and legs but if they chose to pull their legs up, they could quite easily just roll down the street.

Ouch smirked at the stranger beside him, taking in all the sights of his city with his eyes practically on stalks. He resented the boy's presence, feeling that Roland was intruding on his time with Jan. He was beginning to think that Roland seemed like a bit of an idiot – Jan had taken it all much more in her stride on her first visit!

Jan looked at Ouch with a puzzled expression. "I don't remember coming through the city centre before when we went to your cave last time?"

"No, I don't need to go home for anything. All the school pupils are meeting outside the town hall at the end of the street," he replied.

Jan tilted her head for a better view and sure enough, at the end of the street was a small gathering of creatures. Approaching the crowd, Roland stopped and stared in astonishment and fear at a huge three-headed creature that towered above the rest. The first head was an angry-looking bull, the middle head looked like it was made of broccoli and the third head was a Zoogly. The terrified boy gulped when he further saw that these three heads were all joined to a large, dark green, hairy, slug-shaped body.

Roland nervously asked the dragon if there would be a teacher going with them on the school trip. Ouch shook his head to say no, then followed the frightened boy's gaze and saw that he was looking at Cruncher, Muncher and Walleye, a three-headed fuzzbutt monster. Ouch gave a small chuckle and seemed to revel in the boy's uneasiness.

There weren't many fuzzbutts in Zoogly, as they originally came from another planet. This one was legendary both in primary and secondary school. Not only did the creature have the traditional two heads, a meat eating head and a vegetarian head, but it was also born with a rare, additional, third head.

Cruncher, Muncher and Walleye used to be a very mean bully. On Jan's first visit, however, she and the rest of the class had managed to stop the bully right in its tracks; it had never bothered anyone again and had completely turned over a new leaf.

Jan leaned over to Roland to reassure him. "Don't worry, it won't bother you, but remind me to tell you all about the adventure I once had with it when we get home."

Roland grabbed her arm. "Perhaps we should go home now. I don't think a trip in a strange world is one of your better ideas Jan."

"Don't be silly. We'll be fine and anyway, there are worse horrors to face back at school than there could ever be here."

When the crowd spotted Ouch walking towards them with an old friend, shrieks, whoops and shouts of "Look everyone, it's Jan, she's back!" erupted.

Then suddenly, Jan heard a series of noises that she had almost forgotten existed.

"Prrrrrrrrp- Parp- Vadomph! Splat, splat!!"

Her face broke into an enormous grin as she saw her old friend Arty Farty, a loveable and very clever bookworm, amongst the crowd. He was a foreign exchange student and had been one of the pupils she had helped on her first trip, but she had not seen him on her last trip to Zoogly because he had gone home for the summer. Jan noticed he was flirting with a pretty girl bookworm.

Arty did not speak like the others; he made strange noises and unfortunately had very bad breath that puffed out from his mouth in purple clouds when he spoke.

"Oh my goodness Arty, how are you?" She ran over and gave him a big hug. Arty's face lit up as he put his eight sets of arms around her and hugged her closely.

Roland listened to them while they both chatted – well at least he heard Jan speak, and the worm thing seemed to break wind with his face in reply. He did not know that only good friends of a bookworm can understand what they are saying; Jan had earned that privilege by the end of her first visit.

One after the other, the creatures took it in turn to hug her and everyone wanted to know who the stranger was. Jan explained the presence of Roland and they all welcomed him; even Cruncher the bull leaned down for a sniff, which was considered courteous where he came from. Any friend of Jan's was a friend of theirs!

With the introductions and catch-ups all over, the creatures started to pair up and then get into groups of four. Ouch explained that everyone needed a partner to be able to go on this trip and then they would team up with another pair for safety, each set making their own way to Star Lake. But Ouch seemed to be a bit distressed while he was explaining this and Jan asked him what was wrong.

"Well, you see I'm supposed to be paired up with Oops and she hasn't arrived yet. I'm scared she's changed her mind. What am I going to do Jan?" The poor, nervous dragon started to bite off the ends of his claws and spit them out. One hit Roland right on the forehead.

"Ouch!" the boy shouted.

"What?" Ouch asked.

The two were standing there looking at each other in confusion when all of a sudden Oops, the pretty blue dragon with big yellow eyes that Jan remembered from her first adventure, came swirling down from the sky. "Hold on, I'm so sorry for being late. I nearly ate another one of my little brothers again and I was being told off by my parents. *Phew*, I was nearly grounded this time."

Panting for breath, she straightened her long scaly back and began to bat her eyelashes at Ouch in the form of a very feminine apology for lateness.

"Hi-ya Ouch, are you ready for a fun date at the Lake?"

Ouch smiled nervously and, tripping over his tongue, replied, "Yes, friend Jan brought......I mean, look, Jan's back and she's brought another human. It's her friend."

The teenage female dragon went over to have a closer look at Roland and Jan stretched up to Ouch and whispered, "Don't worry, I get all tongue-tied too sometimes but don't worry. Girls think it's kind of cute!"

"Thanks Jan," Ouch told her, looking a bit more reassured.

Roland was looking very wary of the blue dragon, who was circling him and muttering to herself, "You don't look quite the same as Jan, why is that?"

Thinking that she shouldn't be the only one observing, Roland asked her why her name was Oops and what did she mean by, 'nearly ate her little brother again?'

"Well that's a funny story, isn't it Ouchy? My name is Oops because that's the first word I said after I hatched. I ate my brother by mistake and my mum gave me a row."

'This is too, too crazy,' thought Roland and wished he hadn't asked.

Ouch came over to the bemused boy. "And my name is Ouch because that's the first word I said when my mum accidentally blew a flame in my face after I had just hatched! It's dragon tradition, you know, we have to be called by our first words uttered at birth." The dragon said it as if the little human should know all about the ways of his kingdom and he looked rather offended that he didn't.

As the others were starting to leave and make their way to Star Lake, it became obvious that travel plans had to be worked out. Most creatures that could fly would do so, and those who couldn't were able to hitch a ride.

It seemed only right that Roland and Jan should fly with Ouch and Oops, so they decided that Jan should fly on Ouch's back and Roland should fly with Oops. Jan had some uneasy memories of Ouch's skills on the ground from her previous adventures; although accomplished in the air his big feet had previously made him clumsy on the ground. They seemed a little more in proportion with the rest of him now though and she wondered if he had more control over them! So despite wondering whether the landing would be a little bumpy, she insisted on travelling with him. She remembered how easily he had coped with his friend Seezer the wolf on his back and was sure that the flight would be smooth.

Jan saw that Roland was scared so she reassured him that it was an experience to relish and guaranteed him it would be something he would never forget!

CHAPTER NINTEEN

Romance at Star Lake

For Jan, the flight was smooth and a wonderful opportunity to hold on tight and cuddle her best friend, but looking across to Roland she could see the face of pure terror!

Both dragons landed together with a loud thud, gripping the land with their large clawed feet. For Roland, who was not a good traveller at the best of times, it was a flight he would never forget all right, and neither would Oops. The blue dragon wiped off the human vomit from the side of her hip.

"You didn't tell me you would be sick! Now I am going to smell like a rotten snotling."

Jan gave a sympathetic look to the female dragon and took a small bottle of perfume out of her pocket. "Try this Oops. It's like flowers in a bottle and it will help take away that dreadful smell."

Oops' big blue nostrils sniffed the container and she smiled. Loving the smell, the happy dragon danced around while pouring the liquid all over herself.

"Smell me Ouchy, go on and smell me!"

While Oops danced around him, Ouch looked over to Jan, who mimed sticking two fingers down her throat, mimicking that she was going to be sick with the blatant flirting display. Ouch burst out laughing but quickly stopped and straightened up when he saw the less than amused blue dragon raising an eyebrow at him.

Oops didn't like what she saw and narrowed her eyes at the pair. She walked over to Jan and said, "Perhaps on the flight back, you should ride on my back Jan. Us being girls and all that, I think we should stick together. And Ouch, you can have that little human boy barf all over you for a change!"

From that moment on, Oops batted her eyelashes and made a fuss over Ouch at every opportunity she could, sticking to him like glue and making sure that Jan was watching.

As they walked towards Star Lake, Ouch managed to snatch a brief moment with Jan, out of earshot of Oops, and said, "I don't understand it. At school she was acting all hard to get and now, well as you can see, she is all over me and I can't get a second with you."

Jan wanted to explain to Ouch that his girlfriend was being a bit jealous but thought better of it as she didn't want to cause any trouble between them.

Ouch turned to the side and smiled at Oops as she had sped up to catch up with them.

"I hope you are not trying to steal my boyfriend away from me, are you Jan? You do know how ridiculous it would be for a dragon and a human to fall in love don't you?"

Both Ouch and Jan's eyes popped open wide and they began to get flustered and red at the very thought of such a silly idea. Then, for the rest of the journey to Star Lake, Ouch seemed to stay away from Jan and it hurt badly.

The two Zoogly moons were setting and the warm colours of orange and red filled the sky near the horizon. Jan and Roland pointed at the lake on their way down the hill towards the water's edge.

"Oh my goodness Jan, look at the reflection on the lake! It's so amazing. Where on earth could you ever see two moons shimmering on water like that?"

Jan confirmed to him how wonderful the sight was then she noticed that most of the others were already down there and saw what appeared to be large, almost transparent bubbles that were held down with vines.

She waited until Ouch passed close to her and grabbed the opportunity to gauge how he was feeling after that very awkward moment earlier on. She asked him what the bubbles were. Roland listened with great interest. He loved anything that involved a new discovery and on Zoogly, everything was.

"The large bubbles you see are where we go to have our first kiss."

Ouch divulged this information as if his simple explanation should be enough, but of course, Roland had to know the inside and outside of everything.

"You mean they're tents, don't you?" The boy looked up at the red dragon as if he had just answered a million-pound question right on quiz night.

"Come on humans. Let's go get a couple of beach eggs and I'll show you." Ouch led them down to the sandy water's edge. Jan followed him feeling a bit happier that they were back now to a normal atmosphere.

Both humans kicked off their shoes and felt the silky sand seep between their toes. Ouch kept a careful eye on Jan to make sure he was guiding her down the sandy embankment safely into the lake. He wasn't bothered about Roland being less than sure-footed though, as he led them wading through clear warm water where strange thick weeds swirled. They climbed over several large, pink-coloured rocks before Ouch found what he was looking for.

"Here we go." The red dragon held up two golf ball-sized cream-coloured eggs. He poked one of his sharp claws through the top and then the bottom of one of the eggs. Putting it up to his lips, he blew out the contents onto a nearby rock. He held the egg up to the moonlight to make sure it was empty, then proceeded to fill his lungs up with air and blow into the egg with all his might. To Jan and Roland's amazement, the egg began to stretch, growing larger and larger until it became the size of two large dragons.

"Now," said Ouch. "We tie the egg down by using these water vines and boulders and in about an hour, the skin of the egg will be rock hard. Once that happens I will cut a long slit down the centre and hopefully, we will have one of the best shelters on the lake's edge. Well, I expect we will."

Jan looked confused. "What do you mean? You don't sound very sure of yourself!"

Oops barged over to them. "Sometimes it can all go drastically wrong and the whole thing can just collapse. But I am sure that Ouch has made us a splendid one, haven't you my dragon mate?"

Roland looked at Jan triumphantly. "See, I told you. It's just a tent!"

Ouch looked a little disappointed that Roland didn't seem impressed. Coming to the defence of her date, Oops stepped between Roland and Ouch. "That's right, it's a tent little human. A nice private tent built for two … dragons! Now why don't you and Jan both go off for a lovely cosy walk together while me and Ouch finish up here. Go on, off you go."

Jan wasn't sure if Ouch really wanted to be left alone with his suspicious admirer. He didn't look like he did, but she couldn't know for sure and she knew better than to come between two blossoming hearts.

Roland, however, liked the idea. "Come on Jan, let's explore!"

So off they went along the edge of the sandy lake, with the warm winds of Zoogly blowing and the soft colours of the sky changing back and forth from red to orange above them.

Roaming round the edge of the lake was fun for a while, discovering new creatures and plant life, but after a while Jan was anxious to get back. She knew she was safe, as only Fairy Forest with its evil little snotlings was a dangerous place in this realm, but still something was drawing her back towards the beach egg bubbles and the dragons. Roland, however, was jumping from pink rock to yellow rock, going further and further out into the lake.

"Best not go too far out Roland, remember, you can't swim."

Roland excelled at most things but this was one area he had never mastered. However, his fascination for all new things was stronger than his fear of the water and the rocks were firm and stable. They were also wet, however, and as Jan called to him he lost his concentration, slipped slightly and gave out a cry for Jan.

Jan, seeing her friend teetering and then falling into the water beside the rock, bolted towards him and bounced off each rock quickly in an attempt to get to him fast. But

87

she misjudged her last jump and ended up in deep water. She hit the warm water with a huge splash and went under, but she quickly managed to pull herself back up again and gasped for air. Jan was a strong swimmer and was not phased by the accident. Treading water and looking around, she saw with relief that Roland had managed to pull himself back up on to the rock so at least the emergency was over. 'Good grief, that was close,' she thought.

Jan began to swim towards her friend so that she could escort him back to the shore, when suddenly, from deep beneath her, something tugged at her leg. Her heart nearly jumped into her mouth with fright and she strained to look down through the water, but couldn't see anything.

There it was again, but this time the grip on her leg held tight and she was pulled under the water at high speed. Rushing bubbles, hair and loose clothing all went up past Jan's face as she was pulled down, deeper and deeper. The terrified girl didn't know how long she could hold her breath for but she feared the worst. She had heard that drowning was a peaceful death but she really didn't want to find that out for sure. Then the rushing motion stopped. Slowly floating, and with her lungs beginning to burn for air, she rubbed her eyes to get a better view of what was before her. Everything was hazy and marred by bubbles. As they cleared, Jan was astounded to see the most astonishing and beautiful girl smiling at her.

Looking further down, she was startled and involuntarily took in a gulp of water as she could just make out that the girl was a mermaid! A long shimmering tail slowly swept back and forth and her very long hair cascaded around her mesmerizing face.

At this point, with the water now going into her lungs, Jan suddenly felt happy and content. She began to fall into a deep sleep, then, there was nothing but darkness.

CHAPTER TWENTY

A tail to tell

Jan woke up with a jolt and sat up quickly. What had just happened? Was she dreaming about mermaids? The spray from a small splash beside her brought her back to reality and she instantly remembered what had occurred. Thank goodness she was still alive!

Looking around, she could see that she was in a dimly lit cave with some sort of pool beside her. Suddenly, there it was again, a little splash. This time, however, it was followed by a giggle. Jan leaned forward and looked into the pool. She jumped as a face loomed up from the depths. Looking back at her from under the water was the smiling mermaid that she presumed had been the one who had pulled her under the water. But where was she and why did the mischievous little mermaid bring her here?

Jan smacked the palm of her hand down onto the surface of the water and the mermaid got such a fright that she came up coughing and spluttering.

"Why did you do that?" she asked Jan resentfully.

"To get your attention. It's very hard to talk through water. Why did you nearly drown me and where am I?" Jan looked cross.

"I would never drown you! I only wanted to have a private talk with you, away from that handsome land merman."

"What merman?"

"The one you were rushing to save when you fell into the water."

Jan's puzzled frown gave way when she realised who the mermaid was talking about.

"You mean Roland?"

The mermaid closed her eyes and swam about the pool, hugging herself and saying Roland's name over and over again.

Jan began to smile. "You like my friend Roland don't you?"

"Oh, he is so attractive! I just wish he had a tail, but that can be easily fixed."

This took Jan by surprise. "What are you talking about? You have more chance of growing legs than Roland has of growing a tail." The thought of Roland as a merman amused Jan.

The mermaid thought about what Jan had just said.

"Yes! That's a better idea! I will get myself some legs."

"And just how are you going to do that?" But the mermaid seemed preoccupied with her thoughts. "Why don't you just come and talk to Roland. I'm sure he will like you. He has loads of books on mermaids and other wonderful creatures. In fact, he's trying to cross a tortoise with a turtle at the moment."

"But we already have them here. There called tort-tuls. Want to see one?"

Jan had an idea. "I tell you what. You take me back to my friend and I will arrange for you to meet him and you can show him your tort-tul. He will just love that!"

The mermaid thought this was a wonderful suggestion and readily agreed. She explained to Jan how she had pulled her down to her underwater cave.

"Just relax and I will pull you back up to the surface. You'll be safe enough with me; you won't need to breathe air and this time you won't fall asleep because you know what's happening now. It's only the first time I pull down a land creature that they go to sleep. I think it's shock or something. Anyway, my name is Moonpool. What's yours?"

A sudden splash in the pool distracted Jan. "Whoa!" she cried out, as she saw a strange-looking turtle kind of thing looking up at her.

The mermaid looked puzzled, then shrugged her shoulders. "All right Whoa, let's go."

And with that, Moonpool grabbed Jan's arm and pulled her into the water. Jan's journey up this time was quite different. As Moonpool had promised, she didn't descend into unconsciousness and felt no need to breathe – or maybe she was breathing the water. She couldn't tell. The water seemed less murky, with far fewer bubbles, and Jan saw some strange sights as they ascended through the depths. It was very dark when they first came out of the cave, but as it got lighter she could make out all manner of strange creatures, which blinked and gaped soundlessly at her.

At the surface, Jan took a deep breath in, filling her lungs with good clean air, and looked around to get her bearings. She saw Roland in the distance; he had managed to make his way back to the shore. Jan quickly told Moonpool that she would meet her later that night by the group of pink and yellow rocks where they had first met and that she would bring Roland. The mermaid, overjoyed, flicked her powerful tail and soared into the air, then turned and dived deep into the lake, leaving only circles of ripples slowly widening to show she had been there.

Jan swam to the shallows and, standing up, she could see Roland and Ouch running towards her.

Roland, scared by his recent ordeal, stayed out of the water but Ouch splashed his way through the shallow water towards her.

"You're all right. Thank King Eon. Where have you been? Oh my, Jan." And the young dragon picked her up and hugged her.

"I'm fine. Don't worry. Put me down and I will explain what happened."

Jan was shivering and needed to dry her clothes so they headed back towards the bubbles. On the way, Jan told the two boys what had happened.

"You mean you actually met a real mermaid?" Roland was more excited than Jan thought he would be and he agreed to meet with her without having to think twice about it.

Oops gave Jan a large blanket to put round her while Ouch held her clothes up and breathed fire to dry them. They were a little scorched but Jan managed to wear them again.

Oops reminded Jan that the party was about to begin and asked if she could thread flowers through her hair. The girl dragon liked the touch and feel of Jan's long, pretty red human hair and she wished she could be a human.

"Do you really?" Jan asked the girl dragon after hearing this. "I would like to be a dragon for a day perhaps, but my mum always says, don't ever try to be anything other than yourself! People should like you for what's on the inside not the outside."

To celebrate the Heart-Pairing event, there was to be a poetry contest and the winner would be allowed to take their partner out on to the lake on a carved wooden seahorse boat for a moonlight supper. Jan agreed that Roland could spend time with Moonpool by himself while she went to the poetry event; she and Roland were never going to be anything more than friends.

Jan thought that this would be a good experience for him because she had always felt that he would enjoy being more than just friends with a girl, even if she was half fish! And maybe, if things went well here, that might give him some confidence to get a girlfriend back in their own world!

Roland was a bit nervous as he and Jan approached the colourful rocks. Jan could see the young mermaid sitting on a rock waving to them. She was surrounded by a blanket of seaweed and was coyly playing with her long hair.

As they got closer, Jan had to squint her eyes to make sure she was seeing right. As the mermaid removed the seaweed blanket from the bottom half of her body, she could see that the mermaid was no longer a mermaid, she had legs!

Roland stopped and turned to Jan accusingly. "I thought you said she was a mermaid. Where's her tail?"

Moonpool jumped off the rock and walked towards them. She was wearing a water grass skirt but she definitely had legs. Pretty shells hung in strands all around her neck down to her waist and in the moonlight, she looked beautiful.

"Hello Roland." She tilted her head to the side and smiled at the boy.

91

Jan's eyes opened wider as she noticed Roland's face becoming a lovely shade of pink. He had the biggest, silliest smile she had ever seen. Although she was desperate to find out what had happened to the mermaid's tail, she could tell that it was time for her to leave. She would just have to find out later! "I'll leave you two alone now and see you back at the party later. All right Roland?"

But the boy was in a trance and could hear nothing. Jan walked away, very pleased at her friend's new-found happiness.

Jan's hair blew around her face like flags as she walked towards the camp fires that were adding to the glow of the orange and red sky. What a nice feeling it was to see her friend find happiness like this. Looking around as she walked along the beach, she could see Ouch and Oops dancing around holding hands. Ouch still didn't look totally happy and Jan's heart skipped a beat as she wondered whether he was going off Oops. For a moment, she imagined what it would be like if she were a dragon, holding onto Ouch and dancing. Perhaps she would be a red dragon too because of her red hair. She remembered how Ouch had said he loved the colour of her hair and how pretty he thought she was. Suddenly, Jan shook her head and the silly thoughts she was having right out of her mind.

"Jan, come and join us. They'll begin the poetry reading soon."

She smiled and ran up the sandy hill towards the many pairs of starry-eyed girls and boys.

The first to read a poem was Cruncher, the bull head of the three-headed fuzzbutt monster. He had fallen for a single-headed Zoogly, so this was going to make for a very unusual relationship, which his two brothers did not look happy about! It was hard to imagine the head of a bull being romantic, but he cleared his throat and with a bellowing snort, looked longingly into the girl's eyes.

"As long as you are there, we can be a pair,

The fact that I have three heads really isn't fair,

But if you agree to be with me, the sight from my brothers I will take,

So they will no longer see us when we date!"

The crowd remained silent. All eyes were on the female Zoogly, waiting for her reaction. She smiled nervously at her admirer, not exactly sure if he was serious about blinding his brothers – and by the look of terror on their faces, they weren't sure either!

Many other readings were particularly scary and some very tender, but at least everyone had had a wonderful time. Jan couldn't help but notice that Ouch and Oops did not enter and when she looked over to them, they were sitting apart.

The last poetry reading was by a boy who had just walked in with a beautiful girl. It was Roland and Moonpool. She was holding Roland's hand and it was very apparent for all to see that they had fallen for each other. Smiling and looking into her eyes, the love-struck boy began his poem.

"No matter how high the mountains are that a mermaid can't climb,

Or how strong the current is that a boy can't swim,

Together our love will conquer any barrier,

Because, like the vast waters blue,

Our Love is eternal...

Our Love is true..."

The immediate noise of cheers and loud hand clapping filled the night air and it was clear that Roland and Moonpool had won the competition. Everyone ushered them onto the boat that already had a bountiful picnic basket on board and off they were sent, sliding onto the silvery water.

Roland looked for Jan's face amongst the crowed and when their eyes met, Jan knew her friend was thanking her for this amazing adventure.

CHAPTER TWENTY ONE

Who's that boy?

Jan yawned. It was getting late and she was tired. They should really think about heading back home to earth. Ouch had told her that she could use the twig the same way to get them back, but she felt sad to leave. It would take no effort at all to warm up the Fire-Tree wishing twig and get home, but it would take a lot more to forget her new-found feelings for a certain dragon.

She reflected on her adventure so far, from the humiliation at the school to Roland's adventure, and quickly putting her finger up to feel the tip of her nose, she realised her spot was gone. Not having mirrors to fuss and check her appearance in meant she could concentrate on just enjoying herself. Life was simple here in Zoogly and she loved it.

Ouch had noticed that Jan had wandered away and was sitting alone by the water's edge. The gentle giant arrived by her side and sat beside her. They smiled at each other.

The dragon gave a familiar and comforting wink with one of his piercing blue eyes. "What are you thinking about, Jan Otters?"

"I've been thinking about what an amazing time I have had once again. I am very happy when I'm in Zoogly, but…."

Ouch finished her sentence for her. "But you want to go home now."

Jan rested her head on his arm and looked up to his face. "I'm only twelve you know, I need my beauty sleep."

Ouch pressed her nose and made a beeping noise. "I'm half twelve and you will never have to sleep to be beautiful."

Jan chuckled. "Sorry, you're half twelve, don't you mean you're twelve and a half?"

"Oh, yes, that's what I mean. Look, here comes Roland."

Roland came bounding up to them and braked sharply, spraying them both with sand.

"Sorry, didn't mean to get you covered but I have something fantastic to show you both." He put his hand deep into his trouser pocket and pulled out an oyster shell. "Wait until I open it."

The excited boy prized open the shell and allowed the pair to gaze on the polished cream pearl inside it.

"Wow that's lovely," Jan said, almost whispering to herself.

She reached out to touch the cultured treasure but Roland snapped the shell closed.

"No, you can't touch it Jan, until you want to change."

"What do you mean? Change into what?" asked Jan.

"Anything you want!" replied Roland.

Jan gave Ouch a sceptical look, thinking that Roland had lost his marbles when he found the pearl.

"No, you don't understand," the boy said, realising that Jan wasn't buying his story. This surprised him, given that anything was possible in Zoogly and Jan, of all people, should know this by now. "You have to think about the creature you want to turn into, or you can take the image of someone you know. Then hold the pearl high above your head and imagine yourself being that creature or person. That's how Moonpool turned herself into a human. She wanted to be human like me."

"Did she give you that one to keep?" Ouch asked him.

"Yes, this one and seven others, enough for us all to turn into something else. She said it was a going away present since I wrote her the best poem in the world. I could have had a tort-tul but this is far better. Jan, do you want to go first?"

Jan thought deeply about this, then shook her head. "No thank you, I'm too scared."

But Ouch, with a strange, excited gleam in his eyes, grabbed the oyster from the boy and said that he would go first. The dragon stood staring down at the shell in his hand.

Roland was getting impatient. "Go on then. What are you going to be?"

Ouch ignored him and looked intensely at Jan. "I am going to be human but not yet. Jan, I think I know a way to help you with your situation back at school. Will you trust me?"

Jan looked puzzled, but if there was one thing she did know for sure, she could trust her dragon. Ouch told Jan that he had to have a talk with Oops about his plan and, as they had both decided that they would just be friends from now on and nothing more, he wasn't sure if she would help. With long strides he trudged heavily up the sand dune towards the blue dragon, who was sitting in her blown up beach egg.

Roland looked at Jan. "I suppose it makes sense that he wants to be a human. I was thinking of changing into a dragon but guess what I am going to be? Go on, guess!"

Jan shook her head and shrugged her shoulders. She was preoccupied with what Ouch was up to.

"Jan, are you listening to me? You're no fun any more.   Shall I just tell you?"

"Go on then."

"I'm going to be a fuzzbutt monster and go back to earth and scare Maxwell Gettem half to death!" Roland flung his head back and laughed a most evil laugh.

Jan was astounded by this new change in Roland. He seemed a lot more confident. 'Obviously, love agrees with him,' she thought.

"No, Roland, revenge is not the way to go and you should know better. Do you really think it's a good idea to mess with magic? What if you can't change back, or worse?"

"Don't be such a worry wart, that's why Moonpool gave me extra pearls, because you need another one to reverse it."

Jan was anxious. "Look, I think we should just go home and leave all this behind us. Remember – we have a life to go back to and people to face!"

Roland knew she was right but he wasn't going to give up his precious magic pearls that easily.

Ouch and Oops came over to join the pair and, sitting down, they unfolded the plan to them. Ouch told them that Oops had agreed to help and they would need four magic pearls for him and Oops to change into humans and back. Ouch and Oops were going to come back with them to teach a lesson to some very nasty people.

Jan wasn't sure at first but the thought of Ouch as a human lured her into the arrangement without much resistance. However, she was slightly concerned. If she had developed a crush on Ouch as a dragon – well, her mind boggled.

As they were getting ready, Roland leaned towards Jan for a private word. "So now it's all right for revenge?"

Jan had been wondering if he would say anything about that. "This is for the both of us and it's the only way we can ever have any kind of life at school after that mean trick they played. And it's not revenge exactly. We're not doing something nasty back to them; it's just showing them that we're not the unpopular, easily humiliated people that they thought we were!"

Roland pinched his brow together in a suspicious manner. He wasn't convinced that that was all Jan desired from this plan.

Jan and Roland gathered cloth to wrap around the dragons for when they changed into humans and Jan cleverly remembered the "Lost Property Box" back in the janitor's closet. When they got there, they would surely find something decent for them to wear that was more in keeping with the human world they were returning to.

They were ready. Roland handed them each an oyster and they went behind the bushes with their cloths. Jan started to bite her nails. What would he look like? Would his human skin still feel hot like his dragon scales and would he still smell like a smouldering wood fire? She had never been so excited and nervous at the same time. Ouch as a boy, it was just too much for Jan to imagine.

A few seconds later, above the bush, Jan saw each of the dragons stretch an arm above their head and from between their grasping claws, sparkling pearl dust sprinkled down.

The precious pearl had disintegrated in their hands and magic poured all over them. It took about two minutes for anything to start happening and the suspense was killing Jan. Suddenly, stars of silver and gold sparkled lightly around them. Then, a strange light mist hissed through the bushes and a few moments later, two human figures emerged, barely visible at first, but their outline became clearer as they approached.

Jan and Roland were no longer the only two people in Zoogly.

Ouch the dragon had become a tall, almost thirteen year-old looking boy with thick, jet black hair. The end of his raven hair was tipped with red flames as if it had been coloured that way by a hairdresser. Jan thought it would fit in very well with some of the hairstyles the boys were wearing at school – very grungy.

His skin was tanned and this intensified his big blue eyes. Jan decided he was very handsome indeed. But somehow she had known that he would be. She also realised that she definitely had deep feelings for this dragon, even before he had become a boy! Not admitting her feelings earlier on must have been because he was a dragon. It was just stupid to have a crush on a dragon for goodness sake but now ... well, what was to stop her now? But he was her best friend. They'd had many adventures together. Why should she be feeling this now? Jan's head was full of questions and she was more than a bit flustered.

Trying to keep her heart from jumping out of her chest, she stepped forward to study his face closer. Yes, this was definitely still her dragon.

The boy and girl dragons agreed to change their names to something more human and Jan chose Derek Pendragon for Ouch, which he liked very much. Oops was called Pearl in honour of the magic that had transformed them, which she also liked very much.

The change from dragon to human took a further ten minutes for the new human pair to come to terms with – having weird smooth skin and hair sprouting from their heads was bizarre, but the hardest things to deal with were the lack of wings, smaller stature and reduction in weight. This left the pair feeling very vulnerable.

"I feel like I could blow away with one good puff of wind, and no wings to help me out!" complained Oops.

Ouch reminded her that it was his friend's vulnerability that had to take precedence here and they quickly got back to the task at hand. After all, in Jan's world they wouldn't have to deal with anything as dangerous as a snotling, for instance, and if Jan could deal with them here, the two human dragons could surely deal with teenagers in Jan's world!

97

Gaining confidence from this thought, Derek boldly explained the first part of his plan to the others. Then, everyone knowing what they had to do, they linked arms as Jan rubbed the twig between her fingers and wished that they were all back in the janitor's closet.

A familiar feeling of falling surrounded them and, held together, they were swept up in a whirlwind of mist. The twister was full of every colour in the rainbow and in an instant, the four were whisked back to earth and put down on the floor of the dark closet.

"Is everyone all right?" Jan had to ask because she could not see very well. Roland told her to hold on and rummaged around beside him. Suddenly a torch light went on and he pointed it to each of their faces.

"What's that?" Ouch cried, pulling his face away from the bright light.

"Oh sorry, it's a torch for light. It will help us find the lost property box."

From outside the closet, crowd noises could be heard and Jan, remembering her humiliation from before, began to feel anxious. What was Ouch's plan? She knew the first part about her opening the door but what was to happen after that? She really hoped her dragon knew what he was in for with these nasty humans out there.

Roland found the box on the bottom shelf and pulled out a black T-Shirt, combat trousers and a pair of trainers. Unfortunately, Ouch's feet were still too big even in his human form so he just squeezed his toes into them. Oops was given a less than attractive dress and shoes but she thought it was wonderful so they didn't argue.

Jan turned to face Ouch after he had put on the clothes. Derek Pendragon stood head and shoulders taller than Jan and was what Jan's friends would call, "very fit indeed!" He leaned down to Jan's ear and whispered, "Time to open the door Jan." A shiver ran down Jan's back but she was not sure whether it was from the fear of facing the school pupils again or from Derek being so close to her face. Sensing her discomfort, the dragon squeezed her hand and said, "Don't worry Jan, I won't let them hurt you ever again."

It was time, or rather; it was still the same time as before they had left for their journey as no time had really passed at all. Jan could still hear the laughter and shouting from outside.

Taking a deep breath, she moved forward and slowly opened the door, standing there on her own at first. As the door pulled back, everyone laughed louder when they saw her but then, from the darkness behind her, came Derek Pendragon.

All noise came to an abrupt halt!

The boys in the crowed transfixed their gaze to the stranger and then, mouths opened in bewilderment. From the girls there were sharp intakes of breath as they admired the handsome lad and mutterings of, "who's he" and "isn't he gorgeous", began to reach Jan's ears. The humiliated little girl from not so long ago was beginning to have the time of her life!

Derek, the tall visitor, laid a protective arm across Jan's shoulder and stared defiantly out to the crowd. Looking down at her, he winked one of his beautiful blue eyes and smiled then faced the front.

"Where is Maxwell Gettem?" Derek cried out to the audience in front of him.

A slightly intimidated but curious dark-haired boy inched forward, suddenly too scared to go far from the protection of the crowd. Derek narrowed his eyes as he peered over the crowd and down to the boy – the students were not a loyal bunch and they quickly stepped back, disowning Maxwell and leaving him high and dry.

"So you are the immature boy that thought up this silly trick. Well the joke is on you."

Maxwell looked from side to side, begging with his eyes for support from his friends, but they had slunk to the back of the crowd.

"Do you know who I am?" The transformed dragon was starting to enjoy this new power and smiled as he waited for an answer.

Maxwell shook his head, shrugged his shoulders and gave a miserable attempt at looking as if he didn't care.

The tall stranger stepped forward a little from the doorway. "My name is Derek Pendragon. I don't go to this school but you should all know that I don't like the way my girlfriend has been treated here tonight."

The girls all looked at each other in astonishment and now it was their turn for a jaw-dropping moment. Ouch motioned behind him for the others to come forward; Roland and Oops came to the door for all to see. Jan was impressed by her dragon's confidence and watched the reaction of the crowd as Derek continued to talk to them.

"You all know Roland behind me here, and this is Pearl, his girlfriend. So you see, we knew about the joke you were playing and I think we can all agree that anyone stupid enough to think that Jan would be interested in Maxwell Gettem is as dim-witted as he is. We played along with your prank, but let me ask you: where is your girlfriend, Maxwell Gettem?"

"Well," the boy began to stammer, "I don't have a girlfriend right now but I bet I could get any girl here if I wanted to. I would just have to snap my fingers and…" But before the silly boy could finish his sentence, boos and hisses erupted from the crowd.

Maxwell looked around at the faces in horror, and with a beaming red face he about turned and bolted out of the building like he had a dragon on his tail! Jan watched as Maxwell finally got a taste of his own medicine, and all the humiliation and pain he had caused her, ran out the door with him.

From behind Jan and Derek, Pearl was starting to feel a bit resentful of the way that Jan was being protected by her once dragon boyfriend. She and Ouch may have decided to just be friends, but it still hurt to see him protecting another girl like this! Keen to put a quick end to this display, she looked over to Roland who was loosely holding the oysters in his hands. She grabbed two of them and started to crumble the sea gems in her hands, throwing the dust from one over Derek's back, without him realising it, while pouring the other over herself.

With his visit to earth a success, Derek Pendragon stretched taller with pride but, as his spine became taught, he was suddenly aware of a very strange sensation. With horror he realised what must have happened, and that he must be starting to change back to his dragon form. A quick glance over to Pearl confirmed what she had done.

Roland ushered Pearl to the far end of the closet to shield her from the outside gazes, although he needn't have worried as all were transfixed on the new school heart-throb.

The scales that covered Ouch's dragon body began to surface from under his temporary human skin and rippled slowly down his back. Deeply saddened at the revelation that he would have to return to Zoogly so quickly, and profoundly grateful that the transformation was beginning on his back where the crowd couldn't see it, he leaned towards Jan's ear to inform her of his impending yet reluctant departure. Even if Derek and Pearl had not been about to change back into dragons, they all knew this moment had to come.

Jan tilted her head and looked up at her pretend boyfriend as he bent towards her. Jan was pained to learn that they would be torn away from each other again – especially with these new-found feelings reeling around her head. But amidst the tumult of emotions the two were experiencing, they both knew it was just the beginning.

As Derek whispered in Jan's ear, they heard many sharp intakes of breath from the crowd. They glanced sideways to see what the commotion was about, but suddenly realised that the crowd thought their sudden intimate closeness meant they were about to kiss!

The bold dragon boy turned his head further to the side and looked out at them, smiled, winked and with a flick of his wrist, pushed the door closed before they could see any more.

Semi-darkness brought the two even closer and it was now Jan's turn to hold her breath. She closed her eyes and allowed her head to lean back as she felt both Derek's hands upon her shoulders, drawing her close to him. Faintly through her eyelids she saw stars and whirling colours lighting up the room. It was just like in the movies, when the girl was about to be kissed and fireworks went off. She didn't realise that this was the magic pearl dust turning Derek and Pearl back into dragons.

A small, soft kiss landed delicately on Jan's cheek and her heart skipped a beat; she felt like the luckiest girl in the world. They hugged in the darkness and both knew that the other was smiling.

Great dragon wings began to emerge from Derek's back and ripped loudly through his shirt, then settled at his side. "A boy with wings, well that's an interesting thought," mused Jan. But the boy began to think like Ouch again as he whispered into Jan's ear, "We will have to go now Jan, but please don't leave it so long before you come and see me again or guess what?"

Jan wrinkled her nose. "What?"

"Derek Pendragon will have to come back for you!"

ABOUT THE AUTHOR

The author of the Jan Otters' Closet adventures is mother of three, Kelly Forsyth-Gibson. Scottish born and living in the city of Aberdeen, Kelly sought inspiration from her daughter Ashleigh to get ideas to write a book when Ashleigh couldn't find anything suitable in her local book stores. It seemed that all the adventure stories were written with boys in mind while Ashleigh wanted a story with the gritty exhilaration of danger and excitement that only boy's books seem to have; she also wanted the usual girly stuff in it too. The two brought their imagination together to develop some of the most exciting stories for children to be released in the United Kingdom.

Kelly is the inventor of a baby safety product that sells world-wide and while developing her own personal dream over ten years decided that hard work, although very rewarding, could never take the place of the quality time she shared with her daughter. Kelly hopes that this book will encourage her daughter to follow in her footsteps and break through all boundaries of the impossible, hoping to instil in Ashleigh the tenacity to start a project and make it the best she can. Three years of hard work has resulted in something that she is proud to present to the world, leaving her mark for her children and grandchildren to read and enjoy, and proving that day dreams come and go but that great imagination deserves to be immortalized in print.

The subjects addressed in the Jan Otters' Closet adventures are lessons for us all and are met with fun and the sensitivity that these life-changing dramas deserve.

Kelly and Ashleigh say, "Writing together has been one of the best things to ever happen to us – and it's only the beginning!"